Returning to Her Master

BJ Wane

Copyright © 2016 by BJ Wane

Published by Stormy Night Publications and Design, LLC.
www.StormyNightPublications.com

Cover design by Korey Mae Johnson
www.koreymaejohnson.com

Images by Shutterstock/MarishaSha

All rights reserved.

1st Print Edition. July 2016

ISBN-13: 978-1535128841

ISBN-10: 1535128844

FOR AUDIENCES 18+ ONLY

This book is intended for adults only. Spanking and other sexual activities represented in this book are fantasies only, intended for adults.

CHAPTER ONE

Marc Taite leaned back against the bar top and took a swig of his beer as he cast a dispassionate look around the room. The small gathering of friends invited to celebrate Jack and Morgan's engagement were having a good time, some taking advantage of the bondage equipment he and Jack set up for the night; others content, for now, to sit around and converse. Satisfied to watch instead of take part, he wondered if his interest and pleasure in the BDSM lifestyle he and Jack had enjoyed indulging in at their mountain lodge would return soon.

He was happy for his best friend, he honestly was, but he could pin the start of his discontent on Morgan's unexpected arrival on their doorstep six months ago and blame the slow decline of his interest in the lifestyle with Jack and Morgan's budding relationship. Jack first met Morgan when he took a summer job during high school and went to work for her wealthy parents, his main job tending their extensive acreage. He had befriended the lonely, neglected little rich girl and grew to care deeply for the woman she became, but his preference for dominant sexual practices kept him from acting on her obvious adult feelings for him until she sought his help and his embrace after breaking off an unwanted engagement.

Seeing the change in Jack since Morgan had accepted his passions and control had been an eye opener, and of late he'd admitted to craving what his friend had found. Although he'd never enjoyed a special bond with a woman like Jack had shared with Morgan for so long, there had been the hint of one almost two years ago.

The pretty young newbie he'd let down without thinking had been on his mind of late, maybe because Morgan's easy acceptance of her own submissive nature and her stunning responses to Jack's sexual dominance despite her naïve innocence reminded him of Cassie. Volunteering for beginner's weekend at a friend's club in Omaha, he had taken one look at the strawberry blonde and experienced an instant jolt of lust. The first time he had felt her damp response to her first spanking, he had known he wanted more with her. He had spent the past two years regretting giving in to the urge to push her, going too far too fast during those three short nights so long ago. Given the fact he lived in Colorado and she lived there in Omaha, odds were nothing would have ever come of their short time together, but the ravaged look of betrayal on her face that last night still haunted him, rising unbidden whenever he watched or took part in a scene that reminded him of her.

A grin tugged at the corner of his mouth as a look of possessiveness crossed Jack's face when Scott Tyler clasped Morgan's head and slowly slid his cock into her mouth. She was naked and seated backwards on Jack's lap, his cock already buried inside her sweet pussy; Jack was allowing her the pleasure of a ménage to celebrate their recent engagement. During the past six months, his friend had kept her more and more to himself, giving Marc only the rare pleasure of her mouth around his cock, his possessiveness of his fiancée a new development both men were still getting used to. But, for Jack as well as him, much of the pleasure of being a dom lay in exploring and reveling in the heights they took their subs to, and tonight, Jack wanted to give

Morgan that ultimate pleasure again.

Marc's smile turned to a full-fledged grin when Jack landed a sharp smack on her thigh and a visible shudder of pleasure went through her plush body. Nothing felt headier than being with a woman who embraced her pleasures, no matter what kink brought them about. The fact that Morgan still tacked on a title such as sir or master more as an afterthought instead of a respectful address often amused both of them. She was a pleasure to live with and a constant temptation as she paraded around in one of Jack's shirts. She had gotten used to him being a spectator when they played, but still blushed when he jacked off while watching them.

His cock stirred as he watched the two of them bring her to climax, Scott using his fingers to torment her nipples as Jack controlled her lower body with a tight clasp on her hips. Marc swore when she came apart under their ministrations, wishing he could drum up more interest in finding a willing partner among their guests and bury his discontent in her body. Turning Morgan on his lap, Jack soothed her shaking body with soft strokes as he whispered into her ear. Their happiness and contentment defined their relationship, a relationship he envied more each day and wondered if he'd ever experience himself.

Turning his back on the room, he leaned his arms on the bar, wrapping his hands around the half empty beer, glad this was a small enough gathering they didn't need a bartender. He had hoped the tour group he'd taken hiking up the mountain earlier today would energize him for tonight, perk up his appetite for the decadent pleasures his friends were feasting on, but his interest remained neutral at best.

Maybe he would see if he could entice a sub out to the hot tub before he returned to their loft on the upper level of their lodge. It might be summer in the Rockies, but when the sun went down the temperature turned cool and the hot tub stayed popular year round. It was his favorite time of year and he loved the outdoor activities their lodge offered both regular vacationers and those people in the lifestyle who visited them for bondage weekends or vacations.

"Not playing tonight?" Scott asked him as he came around the bar and helped himself to a beer from the kegerator.

"Maybe later." From Scott's look, Marc knew his evasive answer didn't fool him. As the sheriff, Scott knew how to read people, a trait he didn't bother to suppress around his friends. "I saw you made our girl happy," he said, changing the subject.

"I can't take the credit, she's easy to please as long as Jack's touching her." Scott gazed back over at the couple then smiled at Marc. "They do complement each other, don't they?"

"Yeah, they work."

"Is that the problem?" he asked with the astuteness of a long-time friend.

Shrugging, Marc gave him an answer as evasive as his feelings. "Who knows? Haven't you ever gone through spells where nothing seems to work for you?"

"Sure, we all have." Smiling over his upraised arm before he took a long swig of his brew, he added, "I'll quit nagging you if that's all it is."

"Appreciate it," he returned in a dry tone.

"I found out something today that should perk you up. The bakery has a new owner and is planning on reopening in about a week."

"Yeah?" Bear Creek's bakery had remained closed since Martha retired and moved to Denver to be closer to her daughter over a month ago. Marc had been going through sugar withdrawal ever since and he salivated at Scott's news. "Who's the new owner?"

"Not sure, haven't met her yet. I just saw her in passing yesterday, a pretty redhead, young. Hope she bakes as good as she looks."

"I'll have to plan a trip into town next week and check it

out," he said, his interest piqued.

"Let me know, I'll meet you for lunch. In the meantime, I see a lonely sub in need of some attention."

Marc watched him stride across the room to one of the single guests with the group, an attractive blonde who took his outstretched hand with a wide smile of pleasure. The sheriff led her to the St. Andrew's cross where she shed her shorts and top without qualm, her rounded body looking enticing as he strapped her wrists and ankles to the apparatus.

With a heavy sigh, he turned from the couple and came to an abrupt standstill, stunned to see a small, familiar figure standing in uncertainty at the entrance. Wide blue eyes clung to him and he could detect both wariness and pleasure reflected in them from where he stood. That familiar look had his gut clenching as his breath left his body. He'd recognize that red-gold hair anywhere, as well as that petite, tight body. Eyes locked on the woman he hadn't seen in almost two years, the one he had sent fleeing from him in fear and distrust. He stood immobile until she took a tentative step toward him, her look remaining uncertain.

"Cassie?" he asked in disbelief when she stopped in front of him. It had been two years, he thought, and his first reaction at seeing her again hit him just as strong, and his desire for her was just as forceful as that first night.

He noticed her the minute she entered the club room with the rest of the beginners. Marc stood up slowly from where he sat, watching with little interest the sexual activities going on in the Omaha BDSM club. He and his partner, Jack Sinclair, owned the Bear Creek Lodge in the Colorado Mountains, a lodge that catered to those with alternative lifestyles, giving them a safe place to vacation and indulge in their passions without judgement from others. The Omaha club was one of several they had frequented before opening their own and they knew a lot of the members. For the last two weeks, they had been making personal appearances at some of the more reputable clubs in the Midwest to promote their lodge and extol the benefits of vacationing in the mountains at a place that not only offered them all the fun activities of a mountain resort, but a safe place to indulge in their alternative sexual kinks if they so desired. This was their last stop before heading home and Marc had been looking forward to returning to the peace and quiet of his mountain. As much as he enjoyed socializing with others in the lifestyle and playing with a willing sub, he was ready for a little solitude. That is until he spotted her.

For the first time, he was glad Jack had promised Wade they would help tonight with the beginners. Wade was a good friend who owned Raven's Retreat, and he ran a decent place any beginner would find a safe haven for their introduction to the lifestyle. Confident his friend had run a thorough check on IDs, Marc made a snap decision about which little beginner he would tutor tonight.

Stepping forward first to greet the small group, his eyes latched onto a pair of bright blue, wary orbs. Not wanting to risk losing her to another dom, he held out his hand, a simple, non-threatening gesture. "I'm Master Marc. Allow me to show you around."

He released a relieved breath he didn't know he'd been holding when she put her small hand in his, her tentative smile revealing her nervousness. He couldn't wait to be the one responsible for changing her wariness to arousal. Nodding to both Jack and Wade, who watched him with knowing smirks, he led her to a small, unoccupied sofa in a relatively quiet corner. "What's your name, darlin'?" Pulling her onto his lap, he settled her so she sat sideways, facing him with her skirt-draped legs over his.

"Cassie."

Marc liked her soft voice but still frowned at her. "Didn't Master Wade instruct you on how to address a dom?" Her face reddened, which delighted him, as did her quick response.

"Uh, yes, sir. Sorry."

"Tonight you're allowed an infraction or two, but don't forget later. How old are you, Cassie?"

"Twenty-five, sir."

He smiled when her eyes widened as one of the regular couples walked by, the dom leading his smiling, sweaty sub by a leash attached to her collar, her bare breasts sporting nipple clamps. "She looks lovely, doesn't she?" he asked, drawing her wide-eyed attention back to him.

"What? Oh, well, I guess, I mean if you think so."

Chuckling, Marc drew her against his chest. "Relax. No one here will bite you, at least not yet, and not if you don't want them to. Now, tell me what brings you here. You seem to be unsure about your interest in alternative sex."

"Well, to be honest, I'm mostly here on a bet. A friend caught me checking out some of this…." her slim hand waved around the busy room, "stuff. The next thing I know, she's pulling up the website for this place and daring me to come tonight. That's her over there."

He followed her pointed finger toward a brunette on the edge of the dance floor, her body gyrating to the fast beat as she flirted with her partner.

"So, you're here out of curiosity, not any desire to explore?" He couldn't explain the disappointment he felt with her honest answer. If she only came tonight because of a bet, chances were she wouldn't last. Indulging in online exploring was a far cry from reality.

"That's how the evening started," she hedged.

"And?" he prompted, encouraged, a flare of hope replacing his disappointment. Cupping her chin, he turned her face up to his, refusing to allow her to hide when she turned away from him.

"I wouldn't mind… exploring a little."

Marc's cock jumped at her shy admission and the light in her eyes when he wrapped his hand around her hair and held her head immobile. "What's your safeword?"

"Cherry," she whispered, her eyes clinging to his.

"I promise, Cassie, you won't need to use it." With that reassurance, he dipped his head and took her lips in a no-holds-barred kiss. Keeping a tight grip on her hair, he wrapped his free arm around her waist and gave her a small taste of what being restrained would feel like. Her first instinct was to struggle, but experience had him prepared for that newbie reaction and he sharply nipped her lower lip to divert her attention and was rewarded when he felt a small shudder rippling through her body. He soothed the sting with a stroke of his tongue before returning to her mouth, pleased when he drew a low moan of pleasure from her and she leaned against him in surrender.

Marc couldn't remember when he had enjoyed a first kiss more. Her lips were a perfect fit for his, her shy responses inflaming him further. At thirty-three, he wasn't a horny teenager who couldn't control his urges, but something about her stirred both his interest and his lust quicker and in ways he hadn't felt in years. When she moaned again and tried to shift closer to him, he knew he'd have to slow down before he laid her out on the sofa and took her right then. Reluctantly, he lifted his mouth from hers, stroking her lower lip before saying, "I think you'd enjoy being tied to my bed, darlin'." When she drew back in alarm, he tightened his arm, adding, "But first, let's see what you respond to."

Rising, he took her hand and walked with her through the room, letting her observe the play, getting a feel for what she might like and not. He had never taken a virgin sub before. All of his partners have been active in the lifestyle and it had only been a matter of picking one whose needs were compatible with his. It was a fun game he enjoyed playing, but of late he had found himself wondering what it would be like to have a steady relationship, a woman who knew him as well as he knew her.

He glanced down at the petite woman by his side, wondering again what it was about her that pulled at him. She wasn't even his type. He preferred bigger women, softer subs he could sink his hard body into. Cassie was slender, and her unbound breasts beneath the sleeveless tank top she wore with her mid-calf pleated skirt were little more than a handful. And yet, he couldn't wait to get her naked, to feel those small nipples in his mouth and her pussy clasped around his cock.

Her indrawn breath and wide-eyed gaze drew his attention to a lighted scene area where a sub lay strapped down over a padded bench, her bare ass on prominent display. A resounding slap on her right buttock from her dom drew a cry from the restrained woman and another gasp from Cassie. When her blue eyes lit with interested arousal, Marc pulled her closer then shifted behind her, bringing his arms around her and holding her against him.

"I could see you there, Cassie," he whispered in her ear as he moved his right hand up to cup her breast. When she pushed against his palm, he tightened around her, running his thumb over her stiff peak with repeated caresses as the bound woman received another swat on her ass.

"I... I don't think so," Cassie murmured on a soft gasp, her eyes fixated on the scene before her instead of shying away, another positive sign.

"You can't picture yourself in her position, allowing me to spank you, or you can't imagine enjoying it like she does? Look close, darlin'. See how wet she is?" He grinned when she flushed beet red, the blush almost obliterating her cute freckles.

"I don't think I'd enjoy being spanked at all, let alone in public," she replied, but she didn't look away from the scene being played out.

"Let's see, shall we?" He pinched her nipple then soothed the tormented bud with more thumb-rubbing caresses. As her breath sped up, he pinched her again, a little harder, her whimper and slight push against his palm both positive, gratifying signs. "Are you wet?" He bit her small earlobe, then laved it with his tongue. "Answer me now."

"Of course not," she denied on an escaped breath, the blatant lie disappointing him more than it should have.

Marc turned her around, his hands firm on her slender shoulders, and glared down into her startled, aroused face. "Don't ever lie to your dom, Cassie. This lifestyle isn't for you if you can't at least be honest about what you like and what you don't. Your body doesn't lie. Do you want me to reach under your skirt to check for myself?"

The poor girl looked around in frantic embarrassment before hissing, "You wouldn't!"

So, the timid little mouse had a little spitfire in her, much to his amusement and pleasure. "I would unless you give me an honest answer or use your safeword."

"Fine," she snapped. "I'm wet. Are you satisfied?"

"Not yet, but I hope to be once I have you under me." The flare of excited heat in her eyes from his blunt, honest reply sent an answering flame of heat straight down to his cock, encouraging him to push her more than he knew he should a newbie. His eyes on hers, Marc took her hands and pulled them behind her, holding them with a firm grip while he lowered the strap of her tank top, baring her right breast with his other hand. The sounds of slapping flesh, heavy grunts, and soft cries came from the couple behind them as Marc lowered his head and wrapped his lips around a taut nipple. When she pushed into his mouth, he knew she was with him, knew watching the other couple had heightened her senses and lowered her guard even though she couldn't admit it.

Switching from lips to teeth, he nibbled on her nipple then bit it lightly before laving the sting with his tongue. He held her breast cupped in his palm, surprised at the soft fullness as he kneaded her plump flesh and suckled her tight, cherry pink nipple. Fuck, *he thought as his cock demanded attention. When had the simple act of sucking a woman's breast turned him on so much? Her soft cries and restless body fueled his desire, and he had to force himself to let go of his delectable treat and pull back a little before he scared her off.*

Her eyes were wide and dazed when he released her, her lip pinched between small white teeth as she expelled her breath on a heavy pant. "You make it easy to forget you're new to this," he sighed, covering her breast. "Come on, dance with me."

The switch from a clamoring, fast beat to a quiet slow tune played into his plans as he drew her unresisting body into his arms. With her in flat shoes, her head barely reached his shoulders, but she still felt just right in his arms. When her arms slipped around his neck, he cupped her buttocks and held her against his groin, letting her feel how much he desired her and where this could lead if she wanted.

Lifting her head, her tentative look couldn't disguise the arousal in those expressive eyes. "Sir?"

"Soon, darlin'. Tell me about yourself, what do you do when you're not accepting dares from your friend?"

"I'm a high school English teacher and I love to bake. What do you do when you're not doing..." she waved her arm around them, "this?"

"I own a vacation lodge in Colorado and do this." He used his head to indicate the room's activities, more pleased with her by the minute. Her shyness and uncertainty hadn't sent her fleeing yet, which he took as a positive sign.

"How old are you, sir?"

Marc lowered his head to her ear, whispering, "Only eight years older than you, Cassie, but decades older when it comes to experience. Are you sure you want to continue this night with me?" As difficult as it would be, he would let her go if she wasn't sure. He needed her to be sure with a desperation bordering on insane, given their short acquaintance.

Cassie gave him a direct look before surprising him with her candid reply. "I wanted you the minute I entered this room and saw you. You haven't done anything to make me change my mind."

Praying he wasn't making a colossal mistake and could contain his more dominant urges, Marc grabbed her hand and pulled her to the stairs leading up to the private rooms, hoping like hell one was available. He knew he was rushing her, moving way too fast for a beginner, but he couldn't seem to help himself. Much to his relief, he found an empty room with a king-size bed he couldn't wait to see her sprawled on. With any luck, he would get her to come so many times tonight she'd be happy to return tomorrow night and be brave enough to try something new.

"Do you trust me, darlin'?" he asked her when he turned back from securing the door to find her chewing her bottom lip.

"I just met you."

Away from the overstimulating sights downstairs, her self-preservation had kicked in, the worried look she cast at the closed door a dead giveaway. "It's not locked. Master Wade doesn't allow locked doors for safety reasons. I assumed you'd want privacy for your first time here. If I'm wrong, we can go back downstairs."

Panic and a hint of excitement crossed her face with the quick shake of her head, that glorious mane of red-gold hair flying around her shoulders. "Oh, no, please, sir. I want to stay here."

"Good enough. Since I don't want to put you in a position where you have to lie to me, I won't ask you again if you trust me. Let me just reassure you that you can. Now, strip." Arms crossed over his chest, his kept his gaze as direct as his order. The instant puckering of her nipples revealed how much his dominance turned her on.

She wasn't a very neat little sub, he thought with amusement as she tossed each garment onto the chair in the corner along with her sandals. When she stood before him naked, a blush tingeing her cheeks, he damn near came in his pants. She had the prettiest breasts, soft and round, nipples a pale pink. The small roundness of her stomach and patch of neatly trimmed red-gold curls between her shapely legs delighted him.

Reining in his lust, he went to the closet and found a spreader bar, just what he needed. Showing it to her, he asked, "Do you know what this is?"

"Y-yes," she stammered. "What are you going to do?"

"I'm going to see if a little pain stimulates you." Kneeling, he attached the cuffs on the end of the bar to her ankles, leaving her legs spread eighteen inches apart. "Relax." Smiling at her, he sat on the edge of the bed and drew her slowly over his lap, adjusting her so her head hung down with her ass propped up. "Comfortable?" he asked, running his hand over her rounded buttocks.

Peering up at him through the cascade of her hair, she sputtered, "No!"

Marc smacked her cheek, admonishing, "No, what?"

"No, sir."

"Let me see if I can take your mind off your uncomfortable position." He smacked her again, a little harder, and then ran one finger down her slit, pleased with the dampness he encountered. "I think you rather like this position." She cried out with the next two smacks, but another check of her pussy revealed her pleasure at the stimulating pain. Alternating between slapping her buttocks and fingering her warm, wet sheath, he brought her to a fever pitch. Her cries were sounds of pain, but when she lifted her ass for each swat, she told him without words she wanted more of that pain and the obvious pleasure it gave her.

Nothing turned Marc on more than the sight of a wriggling red ass, and Cassie's was no exception. Her buttocks warmed under his hand, a heat he found reciprocated in her pussy each time her warm, damp walls closed around his finger. When he felt the ripples of small contractions heralding her climax, he smacked her ass harder while paying attention to her swollen, needy clit. She screamed as she came, her hips grinding against his thighs, her buttocks jiggling along with her spasming pussy.

He waited for her cries to turn to whimpers and her hips to settle then soothed her buttocks with alternating soft caresses and light, palming squeezes while continuing to stroke her pussy. She was so tight he had to work patiently as he slowly slid two fingers into her core, which inflamed him more, made him want to get inside her faster.

Reaching down, he released the spreader bar and turned her over on his lap, cuddling her shaking body against him. Her tears of submission and the pleasure/pain she received from it endeared her to him in a way he hadn't seen coming.

"Tell me, darlin'," he insisted when she had calmed down from what he suspected was the best orgasm she'd ever had, "have you ever come like that before?"

Cassie turned her face into his shoulder, her body still shuddering with pleasure. "No, sir. Never."

"Good girl. For being so honest even though it embarrassed you, I'm going to reward you. Up on the bed now."

She watched him out of wary eyes as he lifted her right arm and attached her wrist to a cuff before moving to secure her left one. She tugged once on the restraints, and a panicked look replaced the blissful afterglow of her climax. But before she could demand to be let go or say her safeword, Marc held her face between his palms and kissed her, using his mouth to soothe her fears. It took only moments for her to relax and begin kissing him back, for her body to strain against his in a silent plea for more.

"Better?" he asked when he lifted his mouth from hers.

"Yes, much, sir."

As he stripped out of his clothes he couldn't explain the desperation clawing at him to get inside her, claim her before another dom discovered what a treasure she was. It made no sense, he thought as he covered her body with his. He was in Omaha for the weekend then returning to his home in the Colorado Mountains. He wanted to return home, eager to get back to the peace of his quiet mountain and away from the bustling noise and constant activity of the big city. His feelings, the panicking sensation of sinking and going down fast every time he looked into her guileless blue eyes made no sense. But as he slid between her legs and into her tight, welcoming sheath and heard her small cry of pleasure, he couldn't stop the out-of-control spiral of sensations bombarding him from all angles.

CHAPTER TWO

"Marc. Am I welcome or would you rather I left?" Heart hammering, Cassie's pulse had begun racing at just one look from the man who had changed her life in several, irrevocable ways.

"What are you doing here?" he demanded, his tone every bit as bitter as the emotions reflected in his eyes. Shock and anger at her unexpected arrival glittered like shards of glass in his green, accusing glare.

It had taken every bit of her nerve to come here tonight and face him, which left her vulnerable and nerveless in the face of his anger. He had changed little in two years and neither had her feelings for him. He still scared her, and he could still arouse her with a simple look from those enigmatic green eyes. She'd never forgotten him, never forgiven herself for fleeing from him like a naïve virgin, and had never come close to experiencing the pleasure he could give her with someone else. Watching the two men with one woman a few moments ago had in fact excited her, a complete reversal of how she had felt when Marc had tried to introduce her to ménage. Her initial response tonight had been shock, but the longer she watched, the more she saw. The men were gentle, their movements coordinated to bring the other woman nothing but pleasure, making Cassie long to be on the receiving end of such focused attention. She could have had that once, from Marc. But she had been too inexperienced to see what he offered her wasn't a betrayal, but a gift.

"You told me once I'd be welcome to visit you anytime if I was ever in Colorado. I'm sorry, I should've called before I drove out here." She turned, needing to flee from the unwelcome look on his face, only to be brought up short by the clasp of his hand on her arm.

With a sigh of irritation, he muttered, "Upstairs with me. Now."

"You said I would always be welcome. Did you mean it?" she got up the nerve to ask him as he led her into a spacious loft apartment at the top of the stairs.

Marc winced. At the time he had meant those words. He would have said anything, done anything, to erase the look of betrayal on her face their third night together. After she had refused all attempts from him to get hold of her after that night, he had resigned himself to having failed at the one relationship that could have mattered to him. Why now? And just what did she want from him? Both questions fueled his annoyance and concern over the impossible position she had put him in.

Releasing her once they entered the loft, he glared down into her flushed, lightly freckled face, and knew right away he was in trouble. Dressed in a short blue skirt with a matching bustier, there was a maturity about her that had been lacking two years ago, and God help him, he found her even more appealing.

"Yes, I meant it. But for God's sake, Cassie! That was two fucking years ago. I haven't heard a word from you since you took my one call and ended it by telling me not to contact you again." He recalled how much those words hurt and hardened himself against succumbing to those guileless blue eyes again, regardless of the temptation.

Cassie knew this would be difficult, but after learning he

was still single, she hadn't planned, she'd just acted. It had taken her two months and a stroke of good luck to get here, and she refused to give up without a fight. "I'm sorry. I should've let you know I was coming, but I didn't want to give you a chance to talk me out of it." Swallowing her pride, she looked at him with earnest openness. "I wanted a chance with you again so much I…" She was hesitant to tell him the extremes she had gone to in order to prepare herself for seeing him again. "I didn't think about how you might feel about seeing me again."

Marc had to fight to rein in his roiling emotions: anger at her for once again throwing his life and his feelings into turmoil; annoyance with himself for discovering he hadn't gotten over their short time together like he thought he had; and royally pissed at finding he could still want her so much he could forgive her without hesitation, ready to pick up where they had left off all those months ago. She wanted a chance with him again, did she? He wondered how much she wanted it, and how much she had matured.

Stepping forward, he backed her against the wall, bracing his hands on either side of her as he stared down into her wary face. "You want a chance with me again, Cassie?" he asked, keeping his tone deceptively soft. "Show me how much you want that chance, how much you want me."

Stunned at how right this felt, how right he felt when his mouth swooped down and took hers in a hard, wet kiss, Cassie sank into him, clung to his voracious mouth, her lips molding to his, her mouth opening without hesitation for the damp exploration of his tongue. Moaning, she leaned into him, her hands clutching his shoulders as she kissed him back with all the longing she'd tried and failed to suppress since seeing him last. When he moved to untie the top of her bustier and bare her breasts, she didn't attempt to stop him, grateful for his quick action. She didn't want either of them to have time to think, only to feel.

He cupped her breasts in his palms, squeezed her plump softness and pinched her nipples into stiff peaks, the acute pleasure spiraling down to her sheath. Dipping his dark head, he sucked her right nipple between his lips, laving it with his tongue and giving the left a tight pinch. She had to grip his shoulders to keep her balance as she gave a slight push toward his mouth, a silent plea for more. Reaching under her short skirt, he ripped the thong from her hips, surprising a gasp from her as he sought her core. She shuddered when he stroked the bare flesh of her labia, his low, guttural tone as much a turn-on as his exploring fingers.

"Fuck. What did you do with those pretty red-gold curls?"

"I heard men like it when women shave there," she whispered, unable to prevent the spread of heated mortification up her face. "I had it waxed a few days ago."

Marc explored the swollen, denuded folds before slipping between them with ease. "You heard right, darlin', but I did like those pretty curls." Relief at finding her sheath soaking wet made him lightheaded and heightened his urgency to feel her slick walls hugging his cock again, but his passion in response to her didn't sit well with him.

Struggling to set aside his irritation at her unexpected arrival, he turned her toward the wall, pulled her hips back and shoved her feet apart. Grabbing her hands, he braced her palms against the wall where his had been. "Don't move." Flipping up her skirt, he swatted her ass as he released his cock before common sense and caution overruled his body.

"Oh, God," Cassie groaned, lowering her head between her arms, lifting her butt for his next swat, embracing the familiar burn, ecstatic her response to the blistering pain was just as she remembered. One hard, callused palm pressed against her stomach while he belabored her buttocks with the other, his swats coming faster, harder, his concentration on her butt exciting, his silence unnerving.

Her sharp cry following a painful slap on the sensitive skin of the under curve of her right cheek echoed in the loft, the harsh intake of his breathing sending a shiver down her spine.

"Please, Marc," she whispered, wishing she could see his face yet glad she couldn't. But her conflicting, roiling thoughts couldn't compete with the pleasurable heat he took his time building across her butt, the throbbing of her abused flesh spiraling between her legs to be reciprocated in remembered pleasure.

Marc could no more ignore her desperate plea than he could continue to ignore his own demanding need. Grabbing her hips with both hands, he sank into her wet heat, the slick, welcome clasp of her vaginal walls and the enticing view of her bright red ass bringing him to a fever pitch in seconds. Giving in to his body's demands, he pounded into her, ignoring the taunting little voice calling him a sap.

Much more than she had ever expected, Cassie met each hard thrust with acceptance, her body convulsing in spasm after spasm of pleasure so fast she couldn't tell when one orgasm ended and the next began. The wall swam before her tear-filled vision as she relished the pleasure she remembered and had despaired of ever experiencing again.

Marc eased his grip on her hips, hoping she wouldn't be sporting bruises there tomorrow. His senses reeled with the force of his climax and he blamed the last few celibate hours watching others for his unwanted response. Pulling out of her snug pussy brought reality crashing back.

"I need a drink," he muttered, turning away from the look of sated pleasure on her face as she turned around, a look he had never forgotten. "Want anything?"

Cassie straightened her clothing and followed him into the gorgeous kitchen that had her salivating at the thought of baking in it.

"I'll have a beer too," she answered when he pulled one out of the stainless steel refrigerator. "Thank you."

Taking the brew, she took a hefty swallow, working to get her still vibrating body and mixed emotions under control as she looked around his space. The open expanse of the den and kitchen appealed to her as did the floor-to-ceiling windows, hardwood floors, and the comfortable-looking leather sofas. Pretty paintings depicting different mountain scenes hung in artful display on one wall and drew her attention.

Needing to move and avoid his probing look a little longer, she walked up to them, admiring the artist's talent. "These are lovely. Someone is very gifted."

"Yes, she is. Morgan did those."

"Morgan?"

"Jack's fiancée. She's the one you couldn't have missed fucking the two men," he clarified with deliberate bluntness, just to see her reaction. When she didn't respond, just continued to peruse the paintings, he found himself needing to know what she thought of what she had seen. After all, she had fled from a similar situation before. "No comment, Cassie?"

Cassie turned back to face him, flinching at the closed, tense look on his face. "No, Marc, no comment. I didn't come here to berate you for your lifestyle or to interfere with any relationships you have going."

"Why exactly are you here? The last time we spoke, you told me not to contact you again." Two years and he could still recall the way his gut wrenched upon hearing those words in her tearful voice.

Downing the rest of her beer, she padded back over to him and set the empty bottle on the counter. Hopping up on a stool, she winced at the pressure on her sore buttocks, doing her best to ignore his knowing smirk as she folded her arms and faced him across the countertop. Leaning against the kitchen island separating them, he let his beer dangle from his hand as he watched her out of steady, unreadable green eyes.

"That was a mistake in a long line of mistakes I made with you, the biggest one being that I jumped into a relationship too soon after that weekend, and I allowed it to go on longer than I should have. I ended it at the beginning of the year." Rick had been nice, treated her well, and genuinely cared for her. But he wasn't Marc, and discovering her needs were no longer satisfied with a vanilla man had been as upsetting as breaking off their six-month relationship.

"I'm sorry," he replied, but she could tell he wasn't, which gave her a sliver of hope.

"Are you really, Marc?" She needed something from him, just a crumb of encouragement that would prove she hadn't uprooted her entire life and added to a long line of mistakes by moving out to Colorado in search of what she had a chance at once and wanted again.

Releasing an exasperated sigh, he ran a hand over his face, feeling the end-of-the-day stubble and then noticed the redness on Cassie's cheeks. He once demanded honesty from her. He needed to give it also, even now, even though he didn't want to. "Hell, no."

Cassie smiled at him, relieved. "Me either. I know that sounds awful, and he's a nice man, but he's…" She stopped short from saying her ex wasn't Marc. Too much information might have him turning her away instead of fucking her up against the wall again.

"Vanilla?" Marc figured that had to be a big part of what had gone in the relationship. Cassie had fled from the reality of her submissive nature, and from him. He suspected she hadn't found it so easy to set aside.

"Yes, which just reinforced what I knew I could no longer hide from. I had more satisfying sex with you in three nights than I had with him in six months." Her admission brought on another heated blush, but she promised herself she would be upfront about everything with Marc if he would give her another chance to explore her submissive side. "I think I logged on to your website at least once a week in the past few months, reassuring myself you were still here. I also researched the area, the towns around here, and the employment opportunities."

When he raised a black brow, took a swig of his beer,

and didn't comment, she took a deep, fortifying breath and continued. "I don't know if I told you or not, but I worked my way through college in a bakery. I've enjoyed teaching, but it's not my first love. When I saw the ad and my offer for the bakery in Bear Creek was accepted, I turned in my resignation."

Marc damn near dropped his beer at her stunning revelation. "You're the one who bought Martha out?" His fondness for sweets from Martha's bakery was well known.

"Yeah. Do you know the place?"

"I have intimate knowledge of everything Martha had made over the years."

Cassie had forgotten nothing about him, including his sweet tooth and she'd hardly been able to believe her good fortune when she found the bakery up for sale. "I think I can appease your sweet tooth. It will give you a reason to come in to town to see me," she hinted, feeling him out.

It seemed they were both floundering with uncertainty on where to go from here, Marc thought, unable to keep his eyes off her. He still couldn't believe she was here, not only here, but here to be with him. He didn't know how he felt about that, if he wanted to go there with her again or not. The remorse and pain of living with the knowledge his actions drove her away before they could see if they had something worth exploring besides great sex was something he never wanted to go through again.

Ignoring her comment, he stated with an abruptness that made her flinch, "I need to get back downstairs. It's Morgan and Jack's engagement party and they will wonder where I ran off to."

"Morgan. Is she someone special to you?" She hated to ask, but she needed to know if she'd made a horrible mistake in coming here. The way his voice softened when he said the other woman's name had the little green monster rearing its ugly head despite hearing of the woman's engagement.

"Yes, but not like you mean. She and Jack are very much in love and committed to each other, and they're both good friends." He almost smiled at the relief on her face. "Come on, I'll introduce you to her. You'll like her."

"Maybe I should head back to town. I don't want to intrude on a private party."

Laughing, Marc set aside his misgivings for now, grabbed her hand, and led her back downstairs. "Darlin', you've already intruded. You may as well stay and enjoy yourself."

Relieved he wasn't ready for her to go, she tried not to feel self-conscious returning to the party without panties, but then she remembered that if anything, she was still overdressed. The dimly lit, spacious room reminded her of the club in Omaha she had returned to after her split with Rick. It had been over three months since she allowed new-to-the-club Master Greg to prepare her for seeing Marc again and her response to the charged sexual atmosphere had never been this strong. She credited her intense response with being near Marc again and prayed once again this wasn't a mistake. By the sixth return visit to the Omaha club, she knew she wanted to embrace her submissive side and knew she didn't want to do it under another master's tutelage.

The pretty, full-figured brunette he led her toward now wore a man's flannel shirt and sat at the bar. Cassie recognized the man the other woman was smiling at as Marc's friend and partner. Jack Sinclair appeared even bigger than when she met him two years ago, and she still found his rugged good looks appealing. The striking contrast between his light hair and dark beard gave him a rakish look, and it was easy to see why his fiancée gazed at him with such desire. As they neared the other couple, she hesitated and held back, as unsure of her welcome with them as she had been of Marc's.

"What's wrong?"

His quick question reminded her how attuned he could be to her every move and look. "Is Jack going to be upset I'm here?"

He might be, Marc thought, but didn't tell her that. She looked ready to bolt as it was. Though he didn't know what or how much he wanted from her, now his shock had had time to mellow he knew he didn't want her leaving until he figured it out. "It was a long time ago, Cassie, and we've put it behind us. Come on." Tugging on her hand, he stopped next to Morgan and then grinned at the surprise on Jack's face. "Jack, you remember Cassie. Cassie, this is Morgan, Jack's fiancée."

"Hello," Morgan greeted her with a warm smile of welcome. "Are you here on vacation?"

"Uh, no. I just moved to Bear Creek. I met Marc a while back and decided to drop in on him," she answered before shifting her attention to Jack. "Hello, Jack."

"Cassie. It's been a long time. How are you?"

Jack's dark eyes were assessing, but kind, which helped her relax. "I'm good. I hope I'm not interrupting your party. Congratulations on your engagement. Both of you."

Morgan laughed. "No, the more the merrier. Come sit by me and tell me how you know Marc."

"Can I get you something, Cassie?" Jack asked.

She asked for another beer and then sipped this one more slowly than the last while she visited with Morgan. Jack and Marc had their heads together, talking in hushed tones she strained to hear but couldn't. She tried to ignore the way their eyes shifted to her periodically, but with her nerves already shot, it proved impossible to do. A cry from the chain station drew their attention.

"That's Jan," Morgan said, grinning. "Jeremy likes to make her wait for her orgasms so when she's finally allowed to come, she really let's go."

"I had a dom who made me wait, and I hated it. That is until I came. Then I understood the advantages of holding back." Cassie could have bitten her tongue at the startled look on Marc's face. When his jaw tightened and the light in his eyes dimmed, she knew she made a mistake in not ensuring he hadn't heard her.

Marc could kick himself for succumbing to her like a lovesick fool, for even considering taking up with her again. That damning statement proved she hadn't fled the lifestyle all those years ago, only him. Which made a lie out of why she was here. "Fuck this," Marc said to Jack before stalking back over to Cassie, snatching her hand, and pulling her from the room. Out in the lobby, he dropped her hand as if burned. "What's the matter, Cassie? Did your last dom ditch you and you couldn't find anyone local to replace him? What did you think, that I'd be so happy to see you after all this time I'd drop everything and pick up where we left off?" he bit out, not bothering to hide his bitter disappointment and ignoring the threat of tears hovering in her eyes.

"No, it was nothing like that, Marc. Greg, Master Greg, was my only dom since you, and I sought him out because of you." How could she explain to him the utter failure of her previous relationship, her inability to reach the plateau of pleasure she reached with him, and her need to discover if it was the domination she craved so much or the dom? But the quick fuck against the wall earlier told her everything she needed to know. She hadn't come like that since the last time he fucked her and now she knew for sure it was him she wanted, and she had made the biggest mistake of her life when she ran from him so long ago.

"Because of me? You ran from me and what I wanted from you only to end up right back there with someone else. You don't know what you want. Go home, Cassie." Before he could give in to the hurt shining in her expressive blue eyes, Marc turned and strode back into the club room, shutting the door behind him. Too bad he couldn't shut her out of his mind as easily.

Returning to the bar, he poured himself a bourbon, straight. Before he could down it, a hard hand clamped around his wrist. Glaring at Scott, he snarled, "What the fuck do you want?"

"Your hide if you sent that girl back to Bear Creek after she'd been drinking and while visibly upset." Scott's gray eyes bored into him with combined understanding and accusation.

"Ah, shit." Marc set the glass down and rubbed a hand over his face. "I was so upset I didn't think."

"I'm ready to leave myself so I'll follow her and make sure she gets home okay. If I'm not mistaken, she's our new baker and is living above the bakery, so I know where she's going."

"Well, you know more than I do." Guilt and worry twisted his insides as he thought of Cassie upset and driving in the dark along the winding mountain roads that would take her back to town. Even though she wasn't drunk, she had drunk enough to impair her reflexes if something were to happen. "Call me when she gets there, would you?"

Scott nodded as he pulled out his keys. "Jack told me she's important to you, which is the only excuse you could have for having your head up your ass."

"She *was* important to me at one time. Now, now I don't know what she is."

"Well, if she doesn't make it home in one piece, you'll never know," Scott answered with brutal candor. "I'll call you."

CHAPTER THREE

Flashing blue lights in her rearview mirror had Cassie slowing down and pulling over as much as she could on the narrow road. Blinded by tears, hands shaking and throat clogged with a lump of regret, she figured she had been speeding without realizing it. Taking a deep breath that did nothing to control her emotions, she rolled down her window and looked into concerned gray eyes.

"Oh," was all she could think of to say when she recognized the man who she'd watched getting a blowjob from Morgan earlier.

"Cassie, isn't it? I'm Sheriff Scott Tyler. Are you too upset to drive?"

His kind tone and understanding look in those gunmetal eyes helped ease her tense grip on the steering wheel. "No, thank you. I can make it home."

"I'm headed back to Bear Creek myself; I'll follow you to be sure. These roads can be treacherous if you're not used to them, more so at night. You live above the bakery, right?" At her startled look, he hurried to assure her. "I'm the sheriff, Cassie. I know what goes on in my town."

Cassie knew she overreacted, but she learned from her short time with Master Greg, she couldn't be too careful.

"Yes, I'm in the apartment upstairs. I would feel better with some company on this road." Looking out her windshield, an eerie shiver went up her spine when all she could see was the dark shape of trees lining the narrow road.

"Wouldn't want anything to keep our new baker from opening up soon. You're going to be a popular lady. A lot of people have missed Martha's sweets."

"You?" she asked him, smiling for the first time since leaving Marc's lodge.

"You bet. Go slow, I'll be right behind you."

His wink set her stomach to fluttering, after all he was a good-looking man, but he wasn't Marc. Rolling up her window, she pulled back on the road remembering how she had found Master Greg attractive, and how his kind words and demeanor had hidden his true nature. It wasn't until her sixth session with him that he had revealed his true self, even though she had caught hints of it before then. The best thing to have come out of her return to the club where she first met Marc was the affirmation that Marc was who she'd wanted. Too bad her time with another master had ended just as disastrously as her and Marc's short acquaintance.

Pulling into her reserved parking space behind her bakery, she waved to the sheriff as she got out of her car. Locking the door behind her, she went upstairs to the small one-bedroom apartment, took a quick shower, and fell into bed. She groaned as the soft caress of her sheets over the sensitive flesh of her buttocks renewed the warm tingling from her spanking. Sleep eluded her as memories assailed her, memories of both past and present mistakes.

Cassie entered the club, her eyes zeroing in on Master Marc. Last night it had taken all her nerve to attend the first of three beginner's nights at this popular BDSM club in Omaha. In truth, if her friend, Andrea, hadn't found her researching the lifestyle on the Internet and wheedled her into coming here, she never would have had the nerve to come.

There were more people here tonight, she suspected because it was

Friday. The echo of slapping flesh followed by high-pitched screams of release rent the air, sending a shiver of remembrance rippling just under her skin as she recalled the surprising pleasure she'd experienced from her first spanking.

Last night Master Marc had shown her how the pain of a spanked bottom could arouse her to a shattering climax. Her embarrassment over being spanked soon abated as the pain bled into heated pleasure, throwing her into a maelstrom of sensations, sensations she was already craving again. But not with any dom. She set her sights and her heart on Master Marc. The way his green eyes focused on her made her feel special. She liked to think he saw only her, wanted only her, but of course that was wishful, naïve thinking. When he commanded her in that deep voice, she was helpless to refuse him anything. She craved him as an addict did his drug of choice, which should worry her. He wasn't from here and would leave soon. Nothing could come of spending these few evenings with him, nothing that is except experiencing the supreme pleasure of being fucked by him.

Spotting Andrea sitting at the bar, Cassie joined her before she talked herself out of staying. "Did you think I wasn't coming?" she asked when Andrea looked surprised to see her.

"I thought you'd chicken out," Andrea said. "Where'd you disappear to last night?"

"She was with me."

Cassie swiveled around on the stool, her heart speeding up at hearing that deep voice again. "Hi." She smiled up at Master Marc and damned if her nipples didn't pucker and her sheath didn't clench at seeing him again. Seeing him dressed in jeans and a white shirt with the sleeves rolled up to show his strong forearms sprinkled with black hair, his look deep and probing, she knew he was way out of her league.

"Hi yourself." Cupping her face between his palms, he lowered his head and gave her a devastating kiss.

"Well, I guess that explains why you didn't chicken out tonight."

Andrea's dry voice broke through her befuddled brain and had her pulling back from him. "Um, sir, this is my friend, Andrea." Cassie introduced her hoping she'd go away so she could start playing with Master Marc.

"I hear you're the one I have to thank for making sure Cassie

attended beginner's night. You have my gratitude. Have you found someone to show you the ropes?"

They both laughed at the gleam in his eyes and the double meaning behind his words. "Master Wade wants us to have a different dom each night. He said it would broaden our experience."

"Well, he is right about that, but you'll have to tell him not to bother with finding someone for Cassie." Taking her hand, he helped her off the stool. "She'll be spending tonight and tomorrow night with me. Have a nice evening, Andrea."

Cassie waved to her friend as he led her away. There were a lot of new faces tonight, but she had eyes only for Master Marc. His tight grip of her hand bolstered her courage as he ushered her to an empty sofa, sat down, and pulled her onto his lap.

"What took you so long?" he growled before claiming her lips in another wet, heated kiss.

She liked the impatience in his tone and let his mouth distract her from worrying too much about where she knew this could never go. "Sorry I'm late," she answered him when he released her mouth, her voice sounding as breathless as she felt. "I couldn't get away from work early like I had planned. What are we going to do tonight?" She hoped her question sounded more like a casual inquiry instead of revealing how eager she was to feel his hard cock inside her again. From the gleam in his eyes and the small one-sided smile lifting his mouth, she was sure he knew the truth.

"Looking forward to another lesson?"

"Yes," she admitted, having learned not to evade the truth with this man. "What are you doing?" Pressing her hand to her falling top, she kept it from exposing her breasts as she cast an anxious look around to see if anyone watched. She hadn't realized he loosened it when he slid his hand behind her neck, her attention riveted on her body's instant reaction to his.

Displeasure crossed Marc's dark face. "You agreed to submit to me tonight, did you not?"

Cringing at the disapproval in his voice, she discovered she would do almost anything to replace it with a note of approval. "I'm sorry. You took me by surprise." She lowered her hand, allowing the top to fall and expose her breasts, averting her face as a heated blush stole up her neck.

"Much better."

How could the approval in his voice and eyes have such a profound effect on her? Maybe what was responsible for the warmth spreading through her was his touch as he caressed her bared breasts with one hand and pulled her arms behind her with the other. His tight clasp around her wrists added to the thrill of feeling his hands on her again and it took only seconds for her to forget about the people milling about. In truth, the onlookers seemed to enhance her pleasure, a startling discovery she didn't want to think about right now.

"I love your breasts, darlin', and how they respond to my touch."

Cassie gasped when he dipped his dark head and drew one taut peak into his mouth. The strong suction of his lips followed by the rasp of his tongue had her pushing closer to him in a silent plea for more. When he bit the tender bud then soothed it with a slow stroke of his tongue, her sheath gushed in response, her soft cry drawing looks she refused to meet.

Marc released her nipple with a pop and gave her a heated look. "Some women can come with just nipple stimulation. Are you one of those women, Cassie?"

"I… I don't know." Right now she thought the raw lust reflected on his face alone could make her come.

"Let's find out."

He dipped his head again, latching onto her other nipple, worked it with his lips, teeth, and tongue while alternating between pinching and soothing the other one with those clever fingers. Cassie's breath caught on a low moan, the dual assault on her nipples almost more than she could bear. She tried to cradle his head against her, but the quick reminder of her captured hands had her perspiring in need, her whimpers turning to incoherent pleas.

"Please, please, sir," she begged, rubbing her damp, swollen pussy against the erection poking her. She knew tomorrow she'll be mortified at her public display, but the pleasure he heaped upon her nipples, the way they swelled and throbbed, made her oblivious to everything but his ruthless mouth. "Oh, God," she sobbed, pulsations spiraling straight to her pussy.

The orgasm burst upon her so fast, with such unexpectedness, she *could do nothing but go with it. Grinding down on his hard cock, she cried out in stunned ecstasy as her body bowed with the onslaught ripping through her.*

By the time she came back to her senses, she lay slumped against Marc's bracing arm, gasping for breath and shuddering with small tremors, his mouth now relieving her aching nipples with soft suckles and soothing strokes of his tongue.

"I'd say you're definitely one of those women, wouldn't you?"

"I've never done that before—I mean that's never happened before. Not that anyone's tried, but..." When he threw his head back and laughed, Cassie responded with a giggle. "Sir?"

"Yes, Cassie?"

"Can we go upstairs now?"

Marc lifted her off his lap then stood next to her. "You've just proven you don't mind public play. I want to take you further, which means playing down here tonight."

He wanted to fuck her in public? Her first instinct was to refuse, but the lust shining in his eyes kept her rooted in place, his patience while she considered it going a long way in helping her come to a decision. Not trusting her voice, she nodded, hoping she didn't embarrass either of them if she freaked out.

"Pick a safeword and whenever you say it, we'll stop. But I'm warning you. When I say we'll stop, it means we're through."

"For tonight?" She didn't want to be through with him. Right now she wanted him with such desperation, she'd agree to anything, which she proved.

"No, I mean that'll be it for us this weekend. Do you still want to use cherry as your safeword?"

"Yes, that's fine," she agreed, hoping she could accept whatever he had planned.

She tightened her hand around his, knowing if she let go she might run. Conscious of her bare breasts, she attempted to hold her top up to shield them, but Marc's growled "Cassie" made her drop it. Her nipples were still sensitive, and she knew by some of the smiles cast her way several people had witnessed her orgasm earlier. When he stopped at the same well-lit scene area with the high, padded bench where they had viewed a scene last night, uncertainty assailed her despite the need still simmering in her veins. Did he mean to bend her over, strap her down, and take her here? The thought sent her emotions into a quandary. It was one thing to watch such a scene but she couldn't fathom participating in one.

"Second thoughts, darlin'?"

Just like last night, he mesmerized her with that voice, drew her in with the heated look in his green eyes. She wanted him, wanted to feel his hard cock filling her again so bad she would do this. Her orgasm minutes ago only fueled her desire, had her craving him even more.

He lifted her chin until she saw nothing but his eyes, eyes filled with lust for her. "Trust me?"

As unbelievable as it sounded, she did. It was only their second time together, but he had given her nothing but pleasure-filled fantasies and she couldn't deny her need for more. "Yes."

"Then strip."

His smile of approval went clear to her heart, but his curt order still had her hesitating. She turned to see how many people were outside the scene area waiting to watch.

"Don't look at them, they don't matter. I'm the only one who matters tonight."

When he put it that way, it was so much easier. Turning her back to the room, she shimmied out of her dress, slid her thong off, then slipped off her flat sandals. When Marc moved behind her, shielding her, she relaxed and leaned back against him.

"Good girl. You're so beautiful, darlin'. Have I told you how glad I am that you're mine?"

"No, but I'm glad too, sir."

"Master. Call me Master Marc. I want to hear my title from you."

With his hands caressing her breasts and his thick erection nestled against her butt, she found it easier to obey. "Master Marc, I'm glad I'm yours tonight."

His title fell with ease from her lips, as smooth as the way he leaned her over the padded bench and shackled her arms on each side in cuffs lined with soft padding. The height of the bench left her legs straight, but he didn't allow her even that small amount of privacy. With his booted foot, he shoved her feet apart before attaching cuffs to her ankles, leaving her immobile and exposed.

"Master?" she asked with a nervous quiver after tugging on the restraints and realizing how secure they were.

"I'm right here, Cassie. I won't leave your side. You look stunning, darlin'."

His light caress over her buttocks sent a shiver of longing up her spine before he stepped back. She couldn't see what he was doing, which seemed to add to her arousal, but heard him unzipping the black bag he had been carrying with him. When he moved behind her again, she held her breath, anxious over what he had planned. Not knowing heightened her awareness of him, his movements, and her vulnerable position.

Bending over, he drew her face up and asked, "You enjoyed my hand on your ass last night, didn't you?"

"Yes." It would be ridiculous to deny she got off on spanking after she came apart over his lap, and she liked the approval on his face when she answered him without evasion.

"I think you'll enjoy this paddle as well."

He drew back and a sharp smack landed on her right buttock so fast she didn't have time to assimilate his words, the hot pain drawing a cry of surprise from her. The paddle left a burn covering her entire cheek and just as with his hand, the pain soon turned to pleasure and had her longing for the next swat. It landed with a smart snap on her other cheek, this time the pleasurable pain spreading to her aching sheath.

"What do you think of the paddle?"

Desire for more took her mind off the people milling about, her focus centered on her butt and listening to Master Marc's deep voice. "Yes, I like it," she admitted, glad he couldn't see the bright red blush of mortification spreading over her averted face.

"Good girl. Now ask me for more."

Oh, God, could she do that? His patient silence accompanied the caressing stroke of his palm over her abused buttock, his light touch pushing her need for more. "Please, sir."

The paddle landed again, and then again, her breath releasing on a gasp of relief and pleasure. He smacked her with slow, precise swats, raising a fiery burn on her buttocks that had her pussy weeping in response. Cassie bit her lip to keep from crying, her cheeks turning hot, *swelling along with her need to feel his cock buried inside her. Soon she lay sobbing, begging for more, not knowing if she wanted more of the paddle or more stimulation for her deprived sheath. When he set the paddle down and ran his hand over her burning buttocks, she almost came right then.*

Chuckling, Marc said, "You are a delight, darlin'."

Basking in his praise, she lifted her hips when she felt his fingers run over the damp folds of her labia then slide between them to caress long neglected, sensitive tissues and nerves. Her inability to move heightened her arousal and her need for relief. "Master, please."

When she heard him unzip his jeans, she breathed a sigh of relief. Hard hands gripped her sore buttocks right before he demanded in a guttural tone, "Now, Cassie. Come again for me."

Entering her in one strong thrust, he filled her to the hilt, his girth spreading her tight channel wide. The tight pinch of her clit had her screaming, her vaginal walls clamping around his thickness as she splintered apart. Sobbing, she gloried in the feel of his cock pounding into her, taking her hard and fast, leaving her to wonder how she would ever return to vanilla sex after this.

Those three too-short nights had haunted her ever since she ran out on him the third night. She tried going back to vanilla with Rick and, when that failed, she sought another dom. Her responses to Master Greg told her she got off on the light pain and domination, but her climaxes were still tepid compared to the ones Master Marc had wrought from her. She knew after the first night with Master Greg it was Marc she responded to, but she went back, her plan to get as much experience as she could while she weighed the odds of circumstances working out for her to travel to Colorado.

She found the ad for the bakery by chance after looking through the online Denver paper had become habit every Sunday, and took it as a positive sign. Even though Marc hadn't embraced her with open arms, the way he took her, as if he couldn't control himself, was a heady experience and the only reason she refused to return to Omaha with her tail tucked between her legs. It took months of planning and the mistake of trusting the wrong dom to get here, but she knew for certain what and who she wanted. Not only was she submissive, but it was only with Master Marc she could let go altogether, only with him could she reach those unbelievable heights of ecstasy. He was who she wanted.

CHAPTER FOUR

"Thank you, Mr. Collins." Cassie took her mail from the mailman and handed him a blueberry muffin. "Fresh out of the oven and still warm."

Ed Collins smiled in gratitude. "You spoil me, young lady, but mind you, I'm not complaining."

"It's a small thing compared to you bringing in my mail every day. I honestly don't mind picking it up from my box at the post office." A widower in his sixties, Ed worked part time delivering mail to the residents and business owners in and around Bear Creek. Cassie's own grandfather on her mother's side still lived in Omaha and she missed him. Befriending her mailman helped fill that void.

"I know, dear, but then I wouldn't get to see your pretty smile. And I so enjoy your baking. Thank you. See you tomorrow."

"Chocolate cake tomorrow. See you then." The bell over the door tinkled as he let himself out.

Gazing out her wide front windows affording her a view of Main Street, she watched him smile as he ambled next door to the gift shop. Standing behind the glass-enclosed display case holding the day's concoctions, she thought about how much she enjoyed the side benefit of conversing with the residents of Bear Creek throughout her day. It had been a week since she'd opened for business and Cassie loved her little bakery. She'd kept the original name, Ye Olde Bakery. Although she'd liked teaching, the constant politics and dealing with parents who either didn't show enough interest in their child's education or who were too consistently opinionated and demanding had detracted from the experience. Working her way through college in the bakery department of a large grocery store, she had discovered how much fun she could have with it. She liked sinking her hands into a mound of soft dough, working it with her fingers then shaping it into whatever she wanted, like pie crust, cookies, or tarts. Coming up with new recipes and playing with spices and fillings kept her engaged and stimulated, and hearing daily compliments and seeing the look of pleasure on her customers' faces as they bit into a purchase was all very rewarding.

She didn't know there were any small, individually owned bakeries left, thought they had all disappeared along with quaint towns like Bear Creek. When her constant research of the Denver area and the small mountain towns surrounding the metropolis led her to the sale ad of Martha's place, she couldn't believe the opportunity being handed to her. Escaping the problems plaguing her in Omaha had become crucial for her peace of mind, seeking the one man she couldn't forget essential for any future relationships. Disillusionment with her job coupled with signs she had attracted a stalker pushed aside the last small thread of hesitancy keeping her from looking up Marc again after the way she ran from him.

The bright swath of sunlight brightening her shop failed to keep her mood uplifted after Ed's departure. It had been two weeks since she'd seen Marc and she was trying hard not to let his silence get her down. She realized showing up on his doorstep unannounced after months of no communication had to have been a shock to him. For a short time that night he seemed open to having her here, and he proved he still desired her to the point of leaving her aching for more. She had hoped he'd stop in sometime this past week after she opened, if for no other reason than to sample her treats, but it looked like she would have to come up with plan B to get another chance with him.

With a sigh of regret, she shoved aside the urge to call him and picked up her mail. After thumbing through the ads and setting aside the water bill, she came across a plain white envelope. Her palms dampened with nervousness as she slit open the envelope and withdrew a single sheet of paper. As she feared, the message from cutup newspaper was similar to ones she had received in Omaha.

You Are Mine Come Back To Me And I'll Forgive You For Your Betrayal

Those words jumped out at her, had her stomach churning with nausea as she wondered how he found her so soon. For the first time, she felt true fear of her unknown stalker, not realizing how much she had hoped she would leave him behind when she moved. She wasn't one of those women who could run a successful business while taking down a bad guy single-handed without even breaking a fingernail and admitted she needed advice. The closest, most qualified person was the sheriff who had stopped in a few times to check up on her.

Grabbing the note, Cassie locked the bakery and walked the short distance down Main Street to Scott's office. With the number of full-time residents calling Bear Creek their home less than eighty-five hundred, the town remained a small, quaint, close-knit community of people who looked out for each other. The constant bustling activity of tourists, both summer vacationers and winter skiers, drove the population up exponentially during peak months, and provided the income for most of the residents, but she had been told during even those busier times, she could expect the same friendly ambiance as when the townspeople had their town to themselves.

To her relief, Sheriff Tyler was in his office and the attractive dispatcher and receptionist sent her right in to see him.

"Cassie, come in. Is everything all right?" he asked as he rose to greet her with a wave toward a chair.

His welcome smile went a long way toward calming her nerves and Cassie took a seat hoping she wasn't wasting his time by overreacting. "I'm sorry to just drop in on you, sheriff."

"I've told you to call me Scott. You should know by now we don't stand on formalities around here."

Why couldn't she respond to the deep command in his voice like she did to Marc's? With his collar-length, wavy dark brown hair and piercing gray eyes, he'd draw any red-blooded woman's attention. While her body stirred when she pictured herself submitting to him, her mind and heart just wanted Marc.

"Okay, Scott." Handing him the letter, she said, "I was wondering if there was a way to find out where or who this came from."

Scott took the letter, his eyes turning flint gray as he read it. "When did you get this?" he asked, his tone brusque and all business.

"Just now, in today's mail. About two months ago, I got a couple of similar notes in the mail, but since I was already planning on moving from Omaha, I ignored them." Looking back, she realized that had been a mistake.

"You didn't contact the police, show them to anyone else?"

Cassie shook her head, feeling like an idiot for not getting advice back when the notes first started.

"I don't suppose you still have them?" Scott noted the pallor of her face and her clenched hands. She was trying to hide it, but the note shook her up, as it was meant to.

"No. When I moved, I threw them away." *Another dumb move*, she thought.

"I'll try to get fingerprints off it, but odds are whoever it is used gloves. I'll make sure my deputies are aware of this and between us we'll keep an eye on the bakery and around town for anyone suspicious. But, Cassie, this is a tourist area and strangers are the norm here. Have you told Marc about this?" Scott knew Marc continued to struggle with Cassie's sudden appearance and the best way to proceed with her. This incident may have just settled that dilemma for him.

"No, of course not. I wouldn't bother him with this, especially when he's made it clear he's none too happy I'm here." She didn't like that Scott witnessed the humiliating way Marc ushered her out of his lodge, and hoped he didn't know of their past, but knew she couldn't let embarrassment keep her from getting help.

"You came as a surprise, sweetheart, give him a little slack." Rising, he came around his desk and took her elbow. "Come on, I'll walk you back to the bakery and check out your locks for you. For now that's all I can do other than keep an eye out. Make sure you keep your phone on you at all times. I'll give you my office number and my cell number and you can enter them in your phone."

His calm, take-charge attitude revealed he handled his job with serious intent and had her feeling better already. Walking beside him, she felt small next to his larger frame, as small as she did next to Marc. Both men were a little over six feet and had muscled, lean builds; both could set her pulse to racing and cause her happy places to sit up and take notice. But it was only Marc who aroused a need in her so strong it made her want to drop to her knees and do anything he demanded just to please him. She was just sorry it had taken her so long to come to that realization.

After Scott checked her locks and promised to return with better ones, Cassie started her baking for the weekend rush and tried to put both her stalker and Marc out of her mind for now since she couldn't do anything about either situation at the moment.

•••••••

Marc parked his Tahoe in front of the bakery and took a moment to give himself an attitude adjustment. When Scott called thirty minutes ago and told him about the threatening note Cassie received, he responded with a spate of curses, his first instinct to get pissed because she went to Scott and not him with her fears. Of course, his friend was only too happy to remind him he sent her away without a hint she would be welcomed back. Guilt had replaced anger, but the frustration of staying away from her the past two weeks made him irrational, had him swearing again when he realized his actions were the reason she hadn't turned to him and he had no one to blame but himself.

He didn't know what brought her to Bear Creek, or to his lodge, his mind rejecting her claim she was here to start over with him even though his body welcomed her back with a surge of lust he hadn't experienced in two long years. It'd be insane to start over, crazy to think she had changed and now wanted everything he had been foolish enough to push her toward when he knew she wasn't ready. But he wanted to. He hadn't realized how much until he got Scott's call and the thought of someone stalking her, tormenting her, or possibly doing her harm twisted his insides into a tight ball of fury.

Damn it, he swore. With the constant turnaround of summer guests booked into their cabins, he didn't have time to unravel the knots her sudden reappearance in his life had him tied up in. Waiting until he saw the last of the late afternoon customers leave the bakery, he stepped inside and turned the sign to Closed before shutting the door behind him and locking it.

"Cassie, where are you?" he called out when he didn't see her behind the counter.

"Marc? I'm back here."

Following her surprised tone, he went down a short hallway that led to a small office, the large kitchen, and a storeroom. Hearing frustrated mumbling, he found her in the storeroom standing on a stool and attempting to lift down a large bag of flour. Ignoring the way his cock jumped at the taut stretch of denim shorts hugging her delectable ass, he strode across the room. Reaching past her, he grabbed the bag and hauled it down before turning to glare up at her.

"Get down from there," he ordered, trying and failing to control the frustration in his voice. Even with her hair pulled up in a sloppy ponytail, her face devoid of cosmetics, and a streak of flour smearing her cheek, he found her attractive, his body responding without his permission with a painful press against his zipper. He hadn't seen her in two weeks, but there hadn't been a moment when she wasn't on his mind. He wanted her, which he freely acknowledged, but he still couldn't decide where he wanted to go from here.

Cassie took one look at his scowling face and stepped off the stool. She'd had an awful scare today, had gotten behind on her orders, and now she would have to work late to get caught up. She did not want to get into anything with him right now, no matter how delighted she was at seeing him again.

"I'm down. What are you so pissed about?" Moving around him, she failed to stifle the surge of pleasure rushing through her at his unexpected arrival and went to lift the bag of flour.

Grabbing the heavy sack, he snapped, "Pack some things. You're coming back to the lodge with me."

"What are you talking about? I have work to do. I haven't heard from you for two weeks and you think you can just storm in here and snap your fingers and I'll come crawling? Think again." Her anger at his high-handedness replaced her happiness at seeing him, more so because she wanted to obey that demand in the worst way. She couldn't deny the small spark his ungracious invitation ignited, but suspected his offer didn't stem from any strong desire to pick up where they left off.

"Scott called you, didn't he?" she sighed, disappointed he had sought her out only because of some misplaced notion she needed his protection.

"You should've called me. You trusted me enough to pop in out of the blue after two years, couldn't you trust I'd be willing to help you until this asshole is caught?"

"The sheriff replaced my locks with some sturdy deadbolts and he and his deputies will keep an eye on the bakery. I have his numbers programmed into my phone. I'll be careful. There's nothing else that can be done."

"I don't want you staying alone here, especially at night. Come stay at the lodge. Between Jack and me, you'll be safer there than upstairs."

Cassie sidled around him and crossed the hall back into the kitchen, mulling over what to do. This might be her best opportunity to get close to him again, to show him how much she wanted to explore what they had started in Omaha, how much she wanted another chance with him. She knew she never would have responded with such abandon to a man without her feelings involved, nor could sex, any sex, have left her craving more. The question plaguing her the most was how much more could they have together? With only one way to find out, she moved behind her mammoth work counter and geared up her nerve to pin him down with straightforward candor. "And where will I sleep, Marc?"

She could tell by the look on his face he hadn't thought that far ahead. She had learned how protective doms could be, and figured his only thought in making his offer had been to get her where he knew she would be safe. Until he decided for sure if he wanted to pick up their relationship, the last thing she needed was to live so close to him without the benefit of sharing his bed.

"We have a guest room with its own bath. You'll be comfortable there."

Disappointment swamped her, but she held to her resolve. She hadn't disrupted her whole life to come out here and fail. At least, not this soon. Putting on a false, brave front, she replied, "No, thanks then. I'll stay here." She turned her back on him, the move dismissive, but she should've known that would be akin to waving a red flag in front of an enraged bull. He sped around the counter, clasped her arm, and swung her back around to face his frustrated expression so fast the room spun for a split second.

"Why not? What do you want, damn it?"

"You, to sleep in your bed, with you. I want what I came here for. I've regretted running away from you for months now and want a chance to continue exploring submission with you being the one to teach me." She refused to give him more, didn't want to give him additional leverage over her by revealing her feelings, not until she was sure of them herself.

"What's the matter, darlin'? Your last dom leave you hanging?" he asked, his tone calm, almost polite despite the look in his eyes that accused her of betrayal.

Cassie averted her face, recalling how astute he could be. She couldn't let him know the only things she learned from Master Greg were not all doms are worthy of trust and Marc had been more patient, more tolerant of her inexperience than she gave him credit for.

"I have work to do," she replied, avoiding his questions.

There was no way Marc could leave her here alone. He'd never be able to sleep at night worrying about her. Her ultimatum pushed his buttons, her evasive response to his rude question pissed him off, but the small part of him that had never forgotten her, that had regretted losing the chance to finish what they'd started, urged him to give her what she wanted. The Cassie he remembered never would have had the nerve to challenge him the way she had tonight. That change alone stirred his interest, made him wonder how far she would go to get back into his good graces.

"Are you sure you want to submit to me again, Cassie?

Do you know what that even means?" he asked her, his mouth damn near watering when her nipples puckered under her tee shirt, their pointed nubs more obvious because she wasn't wearing a bra.

"I remember those nights at the club very well," she answered, the look of lust entering his eyes sending a shiver of excitement up and down her spine.

"But we're not in that club and you're not naïve about what I want, what I expect anymore. Are you positive you're ready and willing to go down that road with me again?"

His soft voice increased the shivers down her spine, but she wasn't shivering from fear. Marc wouldn't hurt her; she was convinced of that. "What do you want?" she asked, wishing he'd just take her over again, leave her no time to think, just feel.

Marc grabbed the small stool next to the counter and sat down. "Pull down your shorts and bend over," he instructed, almost hoping she would refuse. Then he'd have a way out of this out-of-control situation. To his surprise, she didn't hesitate to unbutton her shorts, push them down, and lower herself over his lap. He had dreamed of having her ass under his hand again these past two weeks, but his dreams hadn't compared to the reality of having her plush buttocks bared and at his disposable.

"God, Cassie, you've got a gorgeous ass." He couldn't help praising her as he caressed her soft flesh.

Cassie kept her head lowered, biting her lip at the light touch of his hand. Her body responded to her vulnerable position and his stimulating caresses with a gush of cream between her legs. Not even when she was in a club wearing nothing had she ever felt so exposed, as vulnerable as she did now. He kneaded her cheeks and the tight squeezes had her shifting on his lap, a low moan slipping past her compressed lips.

"Please," she whispered, ashamed of her need, but craving something more so bad she couldn't help but beg. She'd waited so long for this.

"You beg beautifully, darlin', just like I remember. Is this what you need?"

He landed a hard smack on her right cheek, raising instant, pulsing heat and she felt his cock harden even more. "*Yes!*" She could no more stifle her cry than she could prevent from lifting for the next swat and almost weeping with the pleasure sweeping her senses from the stimulating pain. His swats sped up, became harder, until he had covered her butt several times. Pausing only long enough to shove her shorts down further, he then aimed for her thighs, raising a throbbing burn along the tops before returning to her buttocks.

"I don't like ultimatums," Marc said, his hand smacking her again, the heat of her flesh reminding him of the warmth of her pussy when she clamped around him. "But I like less the worry I'll have to live with each night if you're here alone." He spanked her twice right in the middle of her ass before dipping between her legs and running his fingers over her drenched, swollen folds.

"Sir," she groaned, and even though he suspected the title slipped out without thought as she arched into his hand, it gave him a moment of unguarded satisfaction.

"I don't think so." Though tempted to give her an orgasm, pleasing her would not suit his purposes right now. Lifting her up, he stood and undid his jeans. With a sigh of relief, he freed his aching cock into his hand, those bright blue eyes filling with awe and unfulfilled desire nearly his undoing.

He managed to hold back by sheer willpower. "On your knees." She once again surprised him with her immediate obedience, sinking to her knees in front of him. "Put your hands behind your back and use only your mouth on me."

Cassie had never seen anything as erotic as Marc slowly stroking his hard cock, the small drops seeping from the slit in his bulbous head a sure sign of his pleasure. Her buttocks throbbed hot and swollen, as did her pussy, and she desperately wanted a climax, but not as much as she wanted him, so she did as instructed.

Bending her head, she closed her eyes, savoring his taste as she wrapped her lips around his girth and took him deep. With her arms behind her, the position was awkward and a struggle to hold, but it didn't keep her from stroking him with her tongue, tracing every ridge before swiping over the smooth crown and tasting his pre-come. When he took control by clasping her head, she took him deeper, hollowing her cheeks and sucking hard. His low groan of pleasure encouraged her, his hands guiding her head helped steady her in the awkward position, enabling her to concentrate solely on pleasing him.

Marc thought she made a beautiful sight with her shorts still down around her knees, her ass bare and red, and her mouth filled with his cock. Unable to hold back any longer, he thrust into her once, twice, three more times before exploding, his release shooting down her throat as a storm of sensations erupted from his balls and left him panting.

She released him with a pop, licking her lips as she looked up at him with a pleased smile. "Did I pass your test?"

He didn't like her smug look, or the little twist her impish grin gave his heart. It wouldn't do to let her know yet how well she did pass. Until he got a handle on her, this stalker, and his own roiling emotions, he wouldn't think of their reunion as anything more than friends rekindling an affair for a brief time, an affair that would be on his terms. "Let's pack a few of your things and get going."

Her face fell as he helped her up and pulled up her shorts. "I can't leave yet. I still have baking to do tonight. It'll take me about two more hours. I can meet you there when I'm done."

"No, I'll wait for you." He wasn't sure how much of his desire not to let her out of his sight came from the need to keep her safe or just to keep her close for his own selfish purposes. Either way, he was staying until she was ready.

CHAPTER FIVE

Cassie had never enjoyed her job more than she did over the next two hours. She thought putting Marc to work would speed things up, but she couldn't have been more wrong. His sweet tooth took precedence over everything else and she spent more time trying to keep his hand from reaching his mouth with one of her concoctions and laughing than she did baking. At last, the final batch of cream puffs went into the refrigerator and the donuts into the display case for the early morning customers. She finished her two custom-ordered cakes, and all that remained was the cleanup, something that took longer since in her struggles to keep Marc from eating all her hard work, they had both made a mess of her kitchen.

"Put that back." Swatting his hand, she tried to keep him from reaching for another brownie, but he snatched his hand back without letting go of the chocolate treat. Instead, he gave her an unrepentant grin, licking the gooey fudge from his fingers.

"I need to set a few ground rules before we reach the lodge; the first and most important being I'm in charge."

She returned his smug look with a narrowed eye glare. She wanted him in charge when it came to sex, liked his control and the thrill it gave her, the extra pleasure she got from not having to think or worry over what he wanted or if she pleased him. But aside from sex, it wouldn't do to let him run roughshod over her. "During sex, you're the boss, I get that, want that." Not wanting to push him when she was so close to getting what she came here for, she left it at that.

"Then we're clear. Are we done? I'm hungry and I'll bet the diner has a huge steak with my name on it."

She gaped at him in surprise. "How on earth can you be hungry?"

"Sex, darlin'. I'm always starving after a good orgasm."

"I wouldn't know," she mumbled, thinking of her own needs and how he denied them.

"Ah, poor baby. Feeling neglected?"

She leveled another glare at him, which only made him smile wider. "I shouldn't have let you have any goodies. You didn't deserve them. Now, help me clean up if you want your steak some time before midnight." As he wrapped his arms around her, she leaned into him for his thorough kiss.

"Oh, I definitely want my steak before then. I'm not through with you tonight and I'll need the protein." With a swat to her ass she felt through her clothes, he added, "Come on. We'll get this place cleaned up in no time."

Forty-five minutes later the kitchen sparkled, Cassie had packed enough clothes and toiletries for a few days, washed up, and now sat in the small family-owned diner down the street from her bakery. Her first time in the fifties-era café, she enjoyed the Elvis Presley oldie, 'Jailhouse Rock' reverberating from the jukebox, the homey, classic red and white checked tablecloths and scenic black and white pictures of Bear Creek. The tantalizing aroma of grilled burgers and steaks had her stomach growling, reminding her she missed lunch today.

After ordering the chicken fried steak special, she glanced across their small table at Marc, her mouth going dry at the sizzling look in his eyes, a look that stirred a different hunger in her and had her eager to get going. The past two weeks without seeing him followed by their heated encounter in her kitchen left her frustrated in more ways than one.

"Tell me about your lodge," she said, yearning to learn more about what he had been doing since they last saw each other. The more she knew about him, the easier it would be to learn where she stood with him.

"It's similar to any other mountain vacation lodge. We have fifteen separate cabins we rent out year round and offer different activities depending on the season."

"I saw some of the activities you offer." Her smile teased, but she wondered if that was the norm for him and Jack.

"You mean Morgan and Jack's engagement party? That was a private gathering with a few of our closest friends. We do cater to BDSM groups from all over and reserve certain time slots for them and equip the cabins and club room accordingly as well as planning outdoor activities in the warmer weather. Other times, our guests are families wanting a vacation in the mountains."

The young waitress returned with their salads, her eyes on Marc as she leaned closer to him than necessary to set his bowl down. "Ranch dressing, right?"

"Right, darlin'. Thank you."

Hating the irrational stab of jealousy poking her, Cassie mustered up a polite expression, thanked her for the salad then resumed their conversation, ignoring Marc's knowing look. "You must stay busy. Are you booked now?"

"You want to know what kind of group we have checked in this week? Just regular folks. But we have a small BDSM group coming in next weekend. I'll expect you to attend the gatherings if you're not working," he warned her, letting her know up front what she was getting into.

"As long as I'm with you, that's fine by me. I mean that."

Their food arrived and their conversation turned to mundane topics until it was time to go. After instructing her to follow him, Marc led the way out of town and back to Bear Creek Lodge. The possessive look that crossed her face when Darla flirted with him pleased him more than it should have, more than he wanted. Between that response and picturing some of the outdoor activities he'd like to indulge in with her had him impatient to get inside her again.

Morgan's soft cries following the distinct sound of slapping flesh greeted them as he ushered her into the loft. Grinning at the blush creeping over her face, he led her to his bedroom. "Bathroom's there," he said, pointing to his left. "You've got five minutes."

A little nervous, a lot excited, Cassie wasted no time using the facilities, eager to get naked with him again. Their quick fuck two weeks ago had been thrilling, but she longed for skin to skin contact. The burgundy and navy color scheme she noted in his bedroom carried through into the large bathroom with its double sink vanity and glass-enclosed walk-in shower. Her body quickened as she pictured the two of them together under the multiple showerheads. She hadn't expected him to welcome her with open arms, but his reluctance to take up with her again, have her in his personal space made it difficult to keep a positive attitude. Leaving the bathroom, she swore she'd make the most out of whatever time he gave her.

His back was to her as he rummaged inside an oak armoire so she took a quick look around his room, her bare feet sinking into plush wine carpeting she knew would be warm in the winter months. Floor-to-ceiling windows bracketed the four-poster king-size bed that dominated the room. Two wide, overstuffed armchairs sat facing a large screen television on the opposite side of the bed, but it was the floor-to-ceiling mirrors covering the other wall that held her attention.

Marc turned, his eyes meeting her wide-eyed look in the mirror. "I like to watch and I want you to see yourself as I do."

His simple, direct statement did nothing to ease the tight

ball of tension knotting her stomach. "I don't think I'd like that," she replied with just as much candor.

"But if I tell you to watch in the mirror, you'll do it, won't you, Cassie?"

Spoken with soft authority, his words were more of an order than a question, one she wouldn't rock the shaky boat they were in over. "Yes, sir."

"Thank you. Now, strip."

Cassie removed her clothes under his watchful eyes and by the time she stood naked before him, her nipples had puckered into tight, pointed peaks and her bare folds glistened with arousal she couldn't hide. His vivid green eyes took in every inch of her before he patted the turned-down bed.

"Hop up, darlin', and lie in the middle."

Her few concerns flew the coop when he straddled her body and raised her right arm to attach a wrist cuff before doing the same to her left. When he ordered her to spread her legs, she couldn't help but look down her quivering body and note the embarrassing way her folds separated along with her legs, revealing the pink wet flesh of her vagina. After he attached cuffs around each ankle, leaving her spread-eagled and vulnerable to whatever he wanted to do, he picked up the other pillow.

"Lift your hips."

His calm instructions brooked no argument and, as before, she found herself grateful for his take-charge attitude. All she had to do was obey and enjoy the thrill it gave her.

Tucking the pillow under her buttocks, he then sat back and viewed his handiwork. Responding to his heated look, her stiff nipples pointed straight up, the soft mounds of her breasts laying softly on her chest. Her long, slender legs lay sprawled wide, her hips elevated, putting her mound on prominent display, her breath quickening when he stared with frank openness at her pink, glistening flesh.

Running one finger down her seam, a small grin tugged

at his lips. "Cassie, darlin', if you don't quit biting your lip, I'll be forced to punish you."

Cassie released her lip, her still sore buttocks clenching in protest. Sucking in a deep breath, she watched him dip his head and take a slow lick up the middle of her slit. Unprepared for the searing heat of instant pleasure, she strained against her bonds in a vain attempt to get closer to him, her hips jerking against his mouth.

With a sigh, Marc moved back and shook his head at her. "I see you're not going to behave." Reaching over the side of the bed, he drew out a middle strap and tightened it over her hips, right above her bare mound. "There, now you have to lie still and take whatever I dish out."

"I need to move," she protested without thought. "I need to... *ouch!*" The sudden sting from his sharp slap on the bare flesh of her labia cut off her words and her breath.

"I know what you need, and I'll give it to you when I'm ready and not before. Now, where was I?" Settling between her legs again, he used his thumbs to spread her pink-tinged folds further apart, fully exposing her.

Combined embarrassment and arousal had her whimpering as he dipped his dark head and soothed the burn from his slap with his tongue before delving inside her. Her first instinct to arch against his marauding mouth met with restraint and sent her arousal soaring. She remembered a similar response when they were together in Omaha, a response she searched for and couldn't find when she returned to that club and agreed to be tutored by Master Greg. Shoving aside memories she wanted to forget, she let her mind and body drift on the pleasure of Master Marc's mouth.

The touch of his lips, the stroke of his tongue, and the nibble of his teeth on the bare skin of her pussy sent her into a storm of ecstasy unlike anything she'd experienced before. It shocked her how much more she could feel without hair and vowed she'd keep herself denuded if this was the reward she got for the pain of waxing. She turned her head from the carnal picture of his face between her tethered thighs, only to encounter the shocking, equally carnal image of herself in the mirror with her hips elevated, all the focus on her uplifted mound. Slamming her eyes shut, she ceased to think as he assaulted her with his tongue, his fingers joining in the fray inside her to bring her to a fever pitch. Stroking that one spot sure to set her off, he rooted out her clit with his lips, drawing on the tight knot of nerves with deep suction. Unable to fight the dual assault, a cry slipped past her compressed lips, her body shaking with repeated, strained attempts to move against him. Small tremors heralding an impending climax rippled through her, built to tight clutches when he inched a finger into her anus. Before she could go over into a full-blown orgasm, he inched back, releasing her clit as he pulled with torturous slowness from her body to leave her shaking in frustration.

"Damn it, Marc, quit teasing me," she cried out and then realized her mistake when he frowned at her. "I mean, sir. I'm sorry, just, please...."

Marc couldn't get mad at her. With her flushed face and labored breathing from frustration, her poor bottom lip would not last if he didn't give her relief soon. Discovering she was as responsive as he remembered was both heady and disconcerting as it made keeping his emotions out of the equation more difficult.

"Nice save. Trust me, I'll give you what you need." Dipping his head, he resumed his feast, tasting her on his tongue as he licked, fingered, and nibbled on her flesh until she came close again before pulling back. He brought her right to the edge of climax over and over again, stopping before she could crest that hill. Her ass was tight, but he worked in another finger, and the way she clamped around them told him she enjoyed anal play.

Releasing her clit once again, he glanced up at her soft cry. Tears of frustration and need streaked her cheeks, tugging at his conscience. Dipping his head, he latched onto her clit again, suckling with hard pulls of his lips and pressure from his tongue while he finger fucked both orifices with deep hard strokes. Her walls clamped around his fingers in a slick vise when he nipped the small bundle of nerves, his mouth filling with her cream as she climaxed. The tight press of his cock against his zipper had him cursing for being so eager to torment her he didn't think to strip before lying down with her.

Her orgasm went on and on, her screams echoing in the room as she convulsed under him. He struggled to bring her down slow and easy, licking her sheath with long, slow strokes as he slipped his fingers from her vagina and anus. Kissing her soft folds then her bare mound, he moved up to her waist where he paused to release the strap before continuing up to her breasts. Giving each nipple a soft kiss, he continued his journey to take her mouth in a slow, deep kiss.

Cassie's lips clung to his, tasting her climax as she shook from her explosive reaction. She had never come like that before and she wasn't sure she would survive it if it happened again. Marc was the only man she had ever allowed to give her oral sex. After she fled from him, she had struggled to find herself and her sexuality. Rick liked different positions, but was a very reserved man and happy with conventional sex. When she had finally given in to her memories and had sought a dom to prepare her to return to Marc, she'd been desperate to find answers for herself. But even after Master Greg had agreed to tutor her, she hadn't allowed him that pleasure. She wanted to keep something just for Marc, a sacrifice she didn't know if he'd appreciate, but now she was glad she had made it.

"You have too many clothes on, master," she told him with an impish grin when his lips released hers.

"Yes, I do." Marc rose, stripped off his jeans then reached for a condom off the bedside table until she shook her head at him.

"I'm on the pill and I'm clean if you don't want to use that."

He hesitated then slipped the condom on before releasing her ankles and settling between her thighs again. "Thanks for the offer, but I don't fuck bareback, ever."

"I understand." No doubt they had work to do in the trust department, she thought, then ceased to think at all when he entered her in one smooth thrust.

"Wrap your legs around me," Marc ordered, his tone brusque with impatience and the deep desire to pass on his cardinal rule and feel her silken walls caressing his bare shaft. Thrusting into her, he took her with deep, hard strokes that built to relentless pounding, pleasure swamping him from head to toe.

Cassie clutched his hips with her legs, locking her ankles on his lower back as she met him stroke for stroke. Unbelievably, she felt the pulses of another orgasm starting and when he reached up and released her arms, she clasped his muscled shoulders and rode out the storm with him. His hard, naked body felt so good against her, his breath hot and heavy in her ear as they strained together to reach a simultaneous climax that left them both damp and spent.

• • • • • • •

"I take it you've had a change of heart," Jack greeted Marc the next morning as he poured himself a cup of coffee and eyed his friend and partner over the rim.

"It's more complicated than that." Early morning sunlight poured in from the windows on the far wall, bathing the great room in a swath of light as Marc flipped pancakes while listening for Cassie to rouse. She had fallen into a deep, exhausted sleep last night, but he hadn't been so lucky. The threat of this stalker had decided the issue of whether he would give in to her request to pick up where they left off before she ran out on him. To both his surprise and irritation, he discovered his feelings still ran too deep for him to turn his back on her. "Scott called me yesterday after Cassie had shown him a note she got in the mail from a stalker. There's no way I would let her handle that alone."

Jack frowned at his combative tone. "You don't have to justify your involvement to me. I of all people know how difficult it is to stay away from a woman you want, one your body wars with your mind over. Hell, if you hadn't nudged me in Morgan's direction and she hadn't pushed me from the other end, I'd probably still be just a friend."

"Instead of fuck buddies?"

Jack returned his smile. "That's my soon-to-be wife you're talking about."

"Yeah, and she'd go for the fuck buddy term without blinking an eye. Where is she?"

"Outside drawing. Said something about catching the sunrise. We heard you and Cassie when you came in. You must've wore her out more than I did Morgan. Is she going to be staying here, then, where it'll be safer?"

He stacked the pancakes on a warm plate before pouring more batter on the griddle. "Yes, but the minx refused to come as my guest. She would only agree if she was in my bed, figuratively and literally."

Jack raised an eyebrow. "She blackmailed you? Did you set her straight?"

"I showed her I didn't like ultimatums, but, between you and me, I was glad she forced the issue, taking the decision out of my hands." It still rankled, but he had to concede it simplified things for now.

"You're just as affected by her now as you were two years ago."

"Yeah, it seems like it."

Marc frowned, wondering why Cassie was the only woman he had ever met who could affect him with such strong emotions. They had only known each other on a personal level for days, yet he felt as if he had known her for years. He knew she bit her bottom lip when nervous or unsure about something. She turned a delightful shade of pink when he embarrassed her, bright red when aroused, and when she came her soft voice turned throaty, loud when she screamed. In between scenes, he would sit and talk with her, giving her time to adjust and come down from the ultimate highs she wasn't used to. During those quiet times, he had discovered she loved omelets with spinach and feta cheese, hated mushrooms, and enjoyed an addiction to dark chocolate. She loved to read and took long walks when she needed time to think. Scott told him how she'd befriended Ed, the widowed mailman, and endeared herself to the town's patrons with her warm smiles and welcoming presence. He knew he still wanted her and if anyone hurt her there was nowhere they could hide to avoid his wrath.

Jack slapped him on the back with a hearty laugh. "Welcome to my world. I'll go call Morgan in."

"I heard the shower come on, so I'll tell Cassie breakfast's ready."

Cassie had just emerged from the bathroom dressed in a calf-length denim skirt and a sleeveless blue blouse when Marc entered the bedroom and her heart did that disconcerting flip at the sight of him. Jittery with morning-after nerves, she reminded herself this was what she wanted, what she had insisted upon.

"Good morning, darlin'. Sleep well?"

She loved the way he called her darlin' in his slow, southern drawl. Sometimes she thought she could come from listening to his voice alone. "Yes, but I overslept. I need to get to work."

"You have time for a quick breakfast. Pancakes are already done, table's set, coffee's hot. Come on." Taking her hand, he led her out to the kitchen where she saw Jack and Morgan already seated at the long counter and digging into their pancakes.

Not knowing how the other couple would feel about her presence, she held back. "I'll grab a donut at work. I need to go."

"And miss Marc's pancakes?" Morgan exclaimed when she saw them. "He put bananas and nuts in them and they're to die for. Come join us, Cassie."

"Well, all right, but I must hurry." She sat next to Morgan at the counter and put a plate-size pancake on her plate, grateful for the other woman's open and welcoming attitude. "These are huge. How do you flip them when they're this big?"

Marc took a seat next to her, stacking three large pancakes on his own plate. "I have a big spatula and a lot of experience."

"So, Cassie, do you fix anything in the kitchen besides sweets?"

"Sorry," she replied returning Jack's hopeful look with a rueful grin. "I can bake up a storm and love doing it, but when it comes to fixing a healthy meal, count me out."

"How the hell did we both end up with a woman who doesn't cook?" Marc complained to Jack.

"Dumb luck. The good news is we no longer have to do dishes."

"Let me warn you, Cassie. They make no effort to keep from making a mess when one of them is in the kitchen. I never had dishpan hands till I came here."

She grinned when Morgan looked at her paint-smeared fingers then at Jack as if it were his fault. "Since I already have dishpan hands from cleaning up my own messes, doing a few more dishes won't matter. That was good, Marc, but I need to get going. Morgan, if you'll do these dishes, I'll clean up tonight." Taking a last swallow of coffee, Cassie hopped down from the stool.

"It's a deal," Morgan answered.

"Hold on, Cassie. Let me grab my keys."

Surprised, she glared at Marc. "Don't be ridiculous. Finish your breakfast. I'm perfectly capable of driving myself to town."

Glaring right back at her, he bit off, "I'm well aware of your capabilities, but this isn't open for discussion. I'll take you to work, Scott or one of the deputies will keep an eye on the bakery while you're there, and I'll pick you up."

Fisting her hands on her hips, she stared at him with

incredulous, growing irritation, not liking this turn of events. She loved his control for sex, but she valued her independence, something she'd worked hard to achieve. "You're right, it's not open for discussion because you're being ridiculous. This jerk most likely isn't anywhere around here. I'm going now."

She didn't get far before he stepped in front of her, blocking her exit. "My way, Cassie. That was the deal."

His soft voice and the muscle ticking in his lean cheek made her wary, but didn't prevent her from arguing. "That was about sex, not about you dictating my every movement and shadowing me night and day."

"When it comes to your safety, it'll be my way. Now, let's go."

"Marc, this is asinine. You have your own work to do. Stay here and do it, I'll be fine." When she made to go around him again, she found herself bent over his muscled arm in a move so fast her head spun in dizzying circles. Squealing, she cried out in mortification when he flipped up her skirt and shoved her panties down, baring her butt to both Morgan and Jack. "Let me go, you moron!" she cried out.

Instead, he swatted her ass with his free hand. "No. I warned you about doing things my way. Now you'll know how serious I am about it." Smacking her again and again, he covered her squirming buttocks with hard slaps that left her ass red and his dick hard.

Cassie's shock at being treated like a naughty child couldn't compare to the quick, stunning arousal sweeping her from the painful burn spreading over her butt, the pulsing heat encompassing her entire backside zeroing down between her legs. Knowing the other couple watched only seemed to add to her arousal. Whimpering in shame, she quit struggling in the hopes he would stop before she embarrassed herself further. If any of them looked close enough, she knew they'd be able to see the dampness coating her lips, testament of her aroused state.

Marc landed a few more well aimed smacks when she quit fighting him for good measure. Her bright red, warm buttocks felt good when he ran his palm in a light caress over her skin. A quick dip between her legs told him all he needed to know. Holding back his smile of satisfaction, he pulled her panties up, lowered her skirt, and lifted her to face him. Tears she refused to let fall brightened her blue eyes, her face flushed from more than embarrassment.

"Now, are you ready to let me drive you to work?"

Keeping her eyes averted from the other couple, she mumbled, "Yes, sir."

"Don't fret, Cassie," Morgan called out before they left the loft. "I've had my share of discipline from these two. You'll get used to it."

Too embarrassed to reply, she hurried down the stairs before turning to glare at Marc. "You spank Morgan also?"

"Once in a while, if the situation warrants it. I'm sure Jack'll get the pleasure of warming your ass before long, especially if you keep arguing with me."

CHAPTER SIX

Cassie's busy Saturday morning kept getting interrupted with plaguing images of herself bent over Jack's lap, as she wondered if she would respond to the pain of his hand as she did to Marc's. When Marc had suggested enhancing her pleasure by allowing Jack to join them the third night they met in the Omaha club, her innocence sent her running from the man she was rapidly falling for, taking his suggestion as a betrayal. Yet now, when she pictured herself being spanked by someone else, with Marc watching, her pussy swelled and creamed with the image. She knew from the few nights she spent tutoring under Master Greg's strict hand she got off on being dominated. She also knew from the sex she had with Marc since arriving in Bear Creek that her strongest climaxes came from his hand, his body, his dominance. Her bad experience with Master Greg drove that point home to her, more so when she realized her desire to look up Marc again hadn't dimmed even after Master Greg showed his true colors and left her distraught over his callous treatment of her. But her instant response to Master Marc and seeing firsthand the pleasure Morgan experienced with two men had her accepting the suggestion of another man touching her with anticipation instead of betrayal.

The bell chimed over the door and she smiled at Susan Boggs, a new customer planning the wedding of her only daughter. "I've got it all ready for you, Susan," she called out before turning to Michelle, her part-time help. "Would you get the bridal shower cake out of the refrigerator, please?"

"Sure. It's really pretty, Susan," the nineteen-year-old said with a smile.

"I know Jenny will like it. She's so excited for her shower tonight."

"After doing the shower cake it had me pumped about doing one for her wedding. I did them all the time when I worked in a bakery in Nebraska and had fun coming up with decorations to match color themes. I'm looking forward to it." She loved seeing her concoctions after spending hours decorating, the visual appearance of her work as rewarding as the taste.

Michelle returned from the kitchen and set the boxed cake on the counter, lifting the lid so Susan could see it. "Oh, it's gorgeous, and you were able to use all six of her colors."

"Having six pastel shades for her colors was a great idea and gave me a lot to work with. I'm working on designs for the wedding cake that will also use all six colors."

"Will you be doing Morgan Tomlinson's cake also? I think their wedding will be in August."

Cassie wondered if she would still be here in two months. She loved her little bakery, liked being her own boss even if it was more stressful, and of course she loved being with Marc again. But his lukewarm greeting at her surprise return followed by his reluctance to have her in his bed despite his obvious concern over her safety wasn't encouraging for anything evolving past a few weeks of reunited sex. He had to feel something for her, at least she thought his overbearing, overprotective attitude concerning her stalker suggested he did. But her manipulations had landed her back in his bed, not his insistence. Now she wondered where she'd be when her stalker was no longer a threat.

"I hope I get to do their cake. I've met Morgan and she seems nice," she replied, omitting how she knew Morgan.

"Have you seen her artwork? She sells it at the gallery. She's quite talented." Michelle handed Susan her change then the cake.

"I saw her paintings at the lodge. They're beautiful."

Susan and Michelle exchanged a secret look then grinned at her. "Be sure you call ahead before going out to the lodge, Cassie," Susan warned with a flushed face. "There are certain groups that vacation there that get pretty wild."

She felt her own face turn rosy when both women smirked, then warm even more when Michelle teased, "I take it you saw firsthand what goes on up there?"

"Uh, yes. Are their activities well known around town?" She found it hard to fathom their BDSM parties being accepted without condemnation.

"Oh, sure," Susan answered as if it was no big deal. "This is a small, close-knit community and we don't have a problem with it as long as it's confined to their property, which it is. Besides, the lodge brings lots of business to town."

Relief eased her mind. Now she didn't have to worry about losing business if details of her sex life ever got out. All she had to worry about was making her business a success, a reluctant relationship, and a stalker. Piece of cake, pun intended.

Worry over her relationship continued to plague Cassie throughout the afternoon, more so than worry over her unknown stalker. Michelle left at three when things slowed down, and Marc wouldn't arrive until six, when she closed until Monday. As she marked down items in the display case that wouldn't stay fresh until then, she brooded. Blackmailing him into allowing her back into his bed wasn't how she had planned getting back into his good graces, and something she hadn't thought through before delivering her ultimatum. She'd been so desperate, she hadn't considered the future consequences. Now she had no way of knowing if he wanted her for herself or if he just wanted to ensure her safety. When they resolved the problem with her stalker, then what? Would he return her to her little apartment upstairs and ignore her again, or would he want to give their relationship a try for real, without her coercion and his doubts?

As Cassie cleaned her kitchen and waited on the few late afternoon customers who always showed up for the marked-down goodies, her mood spiraled from bad to worse. She ended up blaming Marc for putting her in the position of having to force her way back into his bed. If he hadn't been so overprotective and allowed the sheriff and his deputies to do their job, then there was the chance the two of them could have one day worked their way back to each other. As much as she enjoyed submitting to him last night and looked forward to more of the intense sexual satisfaction she seemed to only achieve with him, she wished he was with her of his own accord. Though she should rescind her threat and offer to sleep in the guest room, the thought of returning to a platonic relationship didn't improve her mood. By the time Marc entered the bakery right before six, she wasn't pleased to see him.

"You're early. I'm not ready," she snapped and then regretted it when his welcoming smile turned into a frown.

Striding to the counter, Marc eyed Cassie with a cool, apprising look as he considered her foul mood. His heart had done that funny roll in his chest when he'd opened the door and he'd seen her flushed face smudged with a streak of chocolate, tendrils of her red-gold hair clinging to her damp neck. He had thought of her all day, vacillating between frustration, worry, and lust, which led him to an irrefutable conclusion. Even though her refusal to stay at the lodge unless she was in his bed had pissed him off, he had to admit she would have ended up there eventually, if not sooner, anyway. It seemed when it came to Cassie, he had as much self-control as Jack had with Morgan and he could now sympathize and understand why his friend had kept his distance from Morgan for so long. Although it was too early for him to envision a similar positive outcome for him and Cassie as Jack had with Morgan, he at least wouldn't be left regretting turning her away without giving them another chance.

"Bad day, darlin'?" he questioned, stifling his irritation at her greeting until he heard what the problem was.

"I've changed my mind, Marc," she tossed over her shoulder at him as she strode back into the kitchen.

He followed her, her evasion pissing him off. "About what exactly?" Leaning against the large worktable she began swiping with a damp cloth, he folded his arms over his chest, watching her with close scrutiny.

"About staying at the lodge. I'll be fine here. I'll call Scott and let him know the change of plans." Putting away the butter and milk, she tried to ignore the way his jaw tightened and his green eyes snapped with ire, and the way her buttocks clenched in response.

"And you think Scott and his deputies have nothing better to do than babysit one woman who doesn't have the common sense to accept a simple solution and offer of help?"

She winced at the intentional sarcasm. Making her sound self-centered and foolish increased her irritation, the fact he was right pissing her off. "You're an ass, you know that?" she snapped in self-defense then paled when he got that dom look on his face that said she had gone too far. How had she let her worry over what *might* or *might not* happen make her forget who she was dealing with?

Despite wondering what brought on this change of heart, he'd had about enough of her attitude, especially after the day he had. Stalking around the counter, he pinned her against it, caging her in with his arms braced behind her. "You want to tell me what's gotten your panties in a wad?"

It took effort, but he suppressed a smile when he felt her

body shiver at the soft threat in his voice and bet, from the way her eyes widened and her nipples tightened, it wasn't entirely from unease. She shifted, averting her gaze and saying, "No, I don't."

"Well, that's too bad. You made your choice yesterday and I'm holding you to it." Picking up the wide rubber spatula lying within convenient reach on the counter behind her, he ordered, "Turn around and bend over."

Cassie looked from the spoon to his face, swearing at the lack of control she had whenever he got close to her. How was he able to do this to her with just a look and his body bracketing hers? He wasn't even touching her. Acting perverse had been her only defense against the need for him she couldn't seem to escape from, the need causing her sheath to dampen, her nipples to ache. Noting his dead serious expression about using the spatula on her, she remembered where they were. "No way. Damn it, Marc, this is my business. Someone could still walk in."

"Which is why you'd better comply quick. When you forced your way back into my life and my bed, you knew what I would demand of you. My way, Cassie. Anywhere, anyhow, and anytime I say." Raising a dark brow, he challenged, "Or are you running again? Already."

Her face flaming at his taunt, she turned and bent over the counter. There was no way she would give up yet. She had come too far, sacrificed too much to return to him. When he lifted her skirt and shoved her panties down, she bit her lip, both anticipation and dread filling her.

"This is for snapping at me." *Whack!* He snapped the spatula against her cheek, leaving a bright red mark that drew a soft cry from her he didn't feel guilty over. "This is for not telling me what the problem is." Another whack below the first one.

When a third smack landed, she cried out, "What was that one for?"

"For my pleasure."

Marc pressed his other hand on her lower back, a gentle

reminder to be still as he laid a volley of swats across both buttocks, shifting to the under curve when he had reddened both fleshy mounds. A few hard smacks there followed by two across the top of each thigh ought to give her something to think about the next time she sat down. He was about to give her one more, just for good measure, when they both heard the front bell chime, announcing a customer's arrival.

"Marc, sir, please, I need to go see who it is." She prayed he had finished meting out this punishment. She didn't think she could bear the humiliation if a patron witnessed this.

Leaving her panties down, he dropped her skirt and helped her up. Her red face and watery eyes had his cock stirring, her wariness as she looked up at him satisfying him for now. "Come on, let's get them what they want."

"Hello, Mrs. Davies, Mrs. Griffin. Did you find what you wanted?" She cringed when she saw the mayor's wife and her best friend at her counter. Conscious of her throbbing buttocks and her panties bunched around her thighs under her skirt, she plastered on a smile and prayed they were quick. But if she went by past experience, she could count on them to take their sweet time making their selections.

"Hello, Cassie, and Marc! We knew you wouldn't be able to stay away from the bakery for long even though Martha is no longer running it," Madge Davies said with a beaming smile.

"Well, Cassie tempted me with not only her baking but her pretty blue eyes. How could I stay away?"

At her rude snort, he retaliated by sliding his hand under her skirt and giving her sore ass a tight squeeze in warning. When would she learn, she bemoaned, even though she was grateful for his repositioning shift that blocked the women from seeing anything.

"You always were a flirt. Are these rolls fresh, dear?" Mrs. Davies pointed to some sourdough rolls.

With an audible swallow around the lump lodged in her

throat, she managed not to move in fear of giving the women a view of where Marc had his hand. "Made them this morning." Leaning slightly, she slid open the case to lift the rolls out, trying and failing to ignore the way his hand covering the still stinging marks from the spatula reignited the discomfort. Stifling a gasp, she straightened with the tray then almost groaned aloud when his hand remained where it was, caressing her bare cheeks. "How many would you like?"

"Madge, did you see the potato rolls over here?" Betty Griffin asked her friend, both women oblivious of her desire for them to hurry.

When they moved down the counter, she hissed at Marc, "Stop that before they see!"

Marc looked at her flustered face, saw the arousal she couldn't hide in those expressive eyes, the worried mortification in her uneasy glances. Stepping closer to her side, blocking her even more from the two women, he squeezed her buttock with a simple, succinct reply. "No." His look dared her to argue as he kneaded the fleshy mound then traced over the marks from the rubber spatula. Watching her with a keen eye, he slid one finger down her crack to dip between her moist folds. "I love your pussy," he whispered in her ear. "It's so tight," he delved deeper, "and so warm," he shifted to tease her clit, "and so wet." Swirling his finger in her moisture, he coated it liberally with her juices before sliding back up her crack and moistening the tight rim of her anus.

"Marc," she moaned, then bit her lip when he glared at her. Sending a swift glance at her customers, she added, "Sir. Please stop."

"Cassie, dear, will you give me a deal on these two pies?" Betty asked.

"Yes, Mrs. Griffin. You can have both for the regular price of one," she agreed without hesitation. Right then, with his finger tempting her anus with light, damp strokes, she'd agree to anything to get them out of there.

"Very good. I'll take them and half a dozen of these dinner rolls."

Much to her chagrin, he moved the one step over with her, making it look like he was helping her. Bending again to open the case, she couldn't prevent a shocked gasp when his finger slid into her ass.

"Are you all right?" Mrs. Davies asked as she joined her friend. "You look flushed, Cassie."

"I'm just warm from baking all day." Setting the pies and rolls up on the counter, her desperate attempt to stifle her body's reaction to his probing finger met with failure. "Will that be all?" She cursed her shaken voice and Marc under her breath.

"I haven't made my selections yet," Mrs. Davies said. "Marc, what do you suggest for Jim's dessert tomorrow?"

She gripped the counter when he made a show of looking in the display case as he slipped his finger back down to her sheath, swirled it inside her until a climax threatened her composure and her business, before returning to slide into her tight back hole. Fingering her with slow, shallow dips, he pointed to a few chocolate éclairs.

"Those look good. Why don't you get a few of them?"

"Good choice. Cassie, I'll take two éclairs and four sourdough rolls, please."

Cassie's lip hurt from biting it again, perspiration coating her skin with her accelerated heartbeat. The soft, tantalizing strokes over sensitive nerve endings rarely touched made concentrating on wrapping up their purchases and ringing them up difficult. Thank God everything was down at the end of the counter where the cash register sat and she didn't have to move around a lot. By the time the two women said their farewells and headed out the door with their purchases, she teetered on the verge of climax, unsure how much longer she could hold out.

"Ladies, would one of you mind turning the sign to Closed on your way out?"

"Certainly. You two have a nice day tomorrow. See you

next week, Cassie dear." Betty flipped the sign and shut the door behind her.

"Damn it, Marc," Cassie hissed, turning her head. Before she could continue he had a tight grip of her hair and his lips latched onto hers. Moaning in defeat, she kissed him back, her tongue meeting his as he resumed finger fucking her ass.

"Bend over again," Marc ordered when he released her mouth, the sight of her puffy lip ratcheting his arousal.

He'd gotten her into such a state she never considered resisting. Thankful she had closed the blinds over the front windows when the afternoon sun shone in, she leaned over the shorter counter next to the register. Cool air hit her bare skin as he flipped up her skirt, which did nothing to lower the heat pulsing between her anus and her vagina.

Sheathing himself in a condom, Marc grabbed her hips and thrust into her, the red stripes across her buttocks egging him on. As he ran his fingers over them, she released a flood of moisture over his dick. Chuckling, he pounded into her, burying himself over and over to the hilt, his balls bouncing against her thighs with each plunge. Cassie whimpered then cried out as her pussy tightened around him, drawing out his climax.

"That's it, darlin', come on my cock. Come for me now." Releasing her hip, he spread her cheek and thrust a finger into her anus, setting up a pounding rhythm in her ass matching that in her pussy.

The dual stimulation along with his harsh command proved to be too much for Cassie and she let go, crying out with the pleasure as it ripped through her and sent her spiraling out of control. She had just stopped convulsing when she felt his cock swell with a jerk, his shout fast on the heels of hers. His climax triggered another one for her and she buried her head in her arms and rode out the pleasure, thankful her legs didn't buckle under the onslaught and kept her from collapsing.

"Problem?" Jack asked him as he came into the kitchen to pour a cup of coffee. Turning from the counter, steaming cup in hand, he waited patiently for Marc to answer.

Sighing, he took the last swallow of his tepid coffee before pushing back from the counter and taking his cup to the sink. After rinsing it out, he turned to look at Jack standing next to him, a light of understanding reflected in his dark eyes. "I'm fucked, aren't I?"

Chuckling, Jack's reply lacked any sympathy for his plight. "Yup, 'fraid so if your face this morning is any sign." Slapping him none too gently on the back, he added, "It's not so bad. You'll get used to it."

"Bite me." His grumbled reply lacked any real irritation. He should've known by his first, instant response to seeing Cassie again he was screwed. But he didn't have to like it. What if he gave her what she came looking for and she ran again? He wasn't sure he would handle the regret and remorse too well if he failed her a second time. A person could only take so much failure when it revolved around someone special.

"I'd rather bite Morgan. Look, I was where you're at six months ago and thankfully, I listened to your advice. You and Cassie may not have the years of friendship Morgan and I had before I took the plunge and gave in to her demands, but you have *something*. And that's a good start."

That was true, and it did make him feel better. He didn't plan on letting her out of his sight until he removed the potential threat of a stalker, so he may as well forge ahead and see where he could take them, again. She knew the score this time, had even trained under another dom, something that still rubbed him the wrong way and that they would have to deal with sooner or later. But not today. She was off today, but he wasn't. He and Jack had a scheduled hiking tour slated for this afternoon and that would be a perfect time to introduce her to a little outdoor bondage fun.

"I'd like to guide the first half of the hike to Eagle's Lookout, if that's all right with you."

Jack's smile said he knew what he had in mind. "Good idea. We'll meet you there and bring them back. Good spot, secluded but the potential of being discovered won't be lost on her. Mmm, I think I'll head up there early with Morgan and kill a little time while we're waiting for you. The last of our current guests will check out on Tuesday and our new group will start arriving Wednesday with the last of them checking in Friday. The whole group will be staying for the weekend."

"Doesn't give us much time to equip the cabins and the club room." They always looked forward to entertaining some of their friends who indulged in the lifestyle, but preparing for them was time-consuming. "Are we still planning a lingerie night for Saturday night?"

"Yeah. I sent out emails so they could bring getups with them. We'll also divide them up for a hike so they can play outdoors. Other than that, a few expressed interest in waterskiing and boating and making the trip into town for shopping. They'll be an easy group to please."

"Sounds good. We'll head out around one-thirty and meet you there at three."

"Make some noise in case I lose track of time." Jack grinned at him.

"I'd have to make a lot of noise to be heard over Morgan."

"I'll gag her so I make sure I hear you."

Marc laughed, shaking his head. "Later."

Surrounded by towering pines, their lodge sat secluded away from the individual cabins nestled in the woods. Stepping outside, Marc took a deep breath of the warm mountain air, struck again by the peacefulness of their mountain that appealed to him on so many levels. Having met in the military and done time together overseas in some of the worst, god-awful hellholes on Earth, both Marc and Jack savored every moment they spent in their mountain top retreat. They had worked hard to save enough money for a down payment on the two-story log structure that fit their needs to a T, and they'd never taken the success of their vacation rentals and the amenities it provided them with for granted.

How far he'd come and what he wanted was something he needed to remember when he dealt with Cassie this second time around. Remembering the shocked look of betrayal on her face when she learned he had set up a ménage for their last night of newbie introductions at Wade's club, he still questioned whether she really wanted him, and everything he'd want in return. But what plagued him even more was the way she took off, refusing to talk to him after he had spent two nights stressing the importance of communication. He could still recall with vivid clarity the razor-sharp pain of her silence, how it had sliced through him, hurting him more than it should have given their short acquaintance. How much worse would it be if she pulled the same thing again after spending weeks together?

She braved a huge risk returning to him. Maybe it was time he admitted what he always felt for her, and was feeling, was worth some risk also. He wouldn't, couldn't tiptoe around her or rein in his needs as that would send the wrong message. But he'd remember not to take this time for granted, give her what she wanted, show her what he expected, and hope she meant it when she insisted she could not only handle his demands this time around, she wanted them as much as he did.

Walking around to the grassy picnic area behind the lodge, he found her sitting at a picnic table, watching Morgan paint. The afternoon sun had warmed up the day, and she sat with her head tilted back, her eyes on the easel. Her long red-gold hair hung down her back and her pale skin shone with a rosy tint from the sun. She smiled at something Morgan said and his throat tightened. Maybe he ought to commission Morgan to do a portrait of Cassie. He'd seen several she did for some of the residents and they were excellent. That way, if things didn't work out, he would have something to remember her by. Already just the thought of her running again had him faltering, swearing he'd go after her this time if she put him through that.

CHAPTER SEVEN

"Hey." Cassie smiled up at Marc, wondering at his speculative look. "Something wrong?"

"No, darlin'. Do you have a sturdy pair of tennis shoes?" he asked, eyeing her small sandal-clad feet.

"Yes. Are we going hiking?" She had explored none of the hiking trails since moving here and the afternoon was so pleasant, she couldn't think of anything she'd rather do more except spend time with him.

"Yes. I'm taking a group up to Eagle's Lookout in about thirty minutes and you're going with us."

"Eagle's Lookout?" Morgan glanced up at Marc with a knowing glint in her topaz eyes. "Are we going?"

"You're meeting us there to escort the group back."

Marc laughed when Morgan wasted no time packing up her paints. Cassie looked between the two, wondering what they knew that she didn't. "What's at Eagle's Lookout? Is it someplace special?"

"There are a lot of special places on their property. But don't worry, you'll like them. See you guys up there." Morgan folded her easel and practically skipped inside.

Marc watched her go with a fond smile. She had come a long way in the last six months and now embraced her passions with open abandonment, much to his and Jack's delight. "Come on, Cassie." Holding out his hand, she took it and allowed him to pull her up. "Go change your shoes and I'll pack a few things to take with us."

Cassie marveled at Marc's knowledge as he led her and a group of eight guests through a scenic tour of the mountain. They took their time, allowing him to point out plants and wildlife native to the area, stopping at strategically placed lookout spots with breath-stealing panoramic views of the snow-capped mountains and lush green valleys. Forty-five minutes into the hike they stopped at a clearing and rested, taking time to down water and eat an energy bar.

Listening to his deep voice as he walked in front of her, watching his long-legged stride, his taut buttocks clenching with each step, made it difficult to concentrate on her footing or grasp what he was saying. Even looking up at him now from her perch on a log bench, watching him as he swallowed a bottle of water, his strong tanned throat working with each gulp, sent her pulse rate soaring. Her mouth watered at the sight of him, dressed in jeans, boots, and a tight black tee shirt, her appetite for what he dished out never fully sated. They'd had sex that morning, but she wanted him again. She seemed to be insatiable where he was concerned, something she had no desire to rectify. Her tight nipples and damp pussy ensured she would be ready for whatever paces he wanted to put her through. Recalling the way he had controlled her in the bakery yesterday reminded her it was her mind that had trouble submitting, not her body. It had been the same when she first met him, only this time she would make sure her mind got on board with him all the way.

"What are you thinking, darlin'?" Marc asked when he stooped down next to her, a small grin on his dark face.

"About how I can't seem to get enough of you." Her honest answer took him by surprise, as she meant it to. He might have the upper hand in this relationship, but she had ways of getting her own two cents in.

"That just happens to be a mutual feeling. Let's get going so we can do something about it."

Thirty minutes later they reached Eagle's Lookout and met Jack and a flushed-faced Morgan. The small, tree-shrouded glen had one wide open view overlooking the sprawling valley and lake below, the stunning vista from this height taking Cassie's breath away when she looked down. Logs for seating circled a fire pit, and as she sat next to Morgan she noticed how someone smoothed away the roughness, how the grass grew thick and lush, and the trees kept the sun's heat from beating down on them but still allowed for splashes of sunlight to dapple the copse.

"Why do they switch up here instead of one or both of them taking the group the whole way up and back?" she asked Morgan, biting into another energy bar that tasted good, much to her surprise.

Morgan smirked at her. "It all depends on what other activities those two come up with. From what Jack said, Marc wants some alone time with you while up here, so it was no problem for us to take the short route and meet you. Of course, we've been here awhile because Jack wanted his play time as well."

"I've never had sex outside," she confessed, but the hint of it sent a heated rush sizzling through her veins. "But what if someone comes along?"

"That's part of the excitement, never knowing if you'll get caught. I remember one time… oops, no time now. Jack's ready to head out. Have fun, we'll see you back at the lodge."

Jumping up, she joined Jack as he led the group down another path from the one they came up on. Cassie rose and waved goodbye before turning to see Marc removing his small backpack from his shoulders.

"Cassie, do you need more water?"

"No, I'm good. This is a beautiful spot."

"One of my favorites. Jack and I spent days traipsing these woods and locating different rest areas. Come here, darlin'." Marc sat on a large log and held his hand out to her, enjoying the signs of nervousness and arousal crossing her expressive face. When she stopped next to him, he reached up and unbuttoned her shorts, his eyes never leaving hers. After lowering the zipper, he pulled them down and urged her over his lap. "Bend over. I have a need to feel that soft ass under my hand."

"This is getting to be a habit," she muttered, bending over his hard, jean-clad thighs, the soft breeze fluttering over her exposed butt making her ache for a harder touch.

"One I don't intend to break." He adjusted her so her buttocks lay over his right leg, her hands braced on the ground, head down and knees bent. Perfect. Running a hand over her round, pale cheeks, he waited until her tense muscles relaxed and acceptance took over. "That's a good girl."

His simple praise shook her, left her yearning to please him in all ways. Baring nothing but her ass while they both stayed clothed heightened her vulnerability, left her more conscious of that part of her anatomy and how he might view it. Where her breasts were nothing to brag about, a medium size, her buttocks had more flesh to them. Leaving her trembling over his lap in anticipation while he did nothing but stroke her sensitive flesh kept her teetering on the edge of arousal, holding her breath as she waited for that first smack. When she shifted in anxious unease, the rat bastard just chuckled.

"Do you want something?"

Turning her head, she glared up at him through the curtain of hair sliding over her face, but at his immediate frown she stifled the sarcastic retort begging to be uttered. "Sir, please," she replied instead, giving him what he wanted so she could get what she wanted sooner.

"Master, Cassie. Call me master."

His guttural tone sent a shiver rippling through her, had her answering in a breathless whisper, "Master, please."

"Please what?" he asked, refusing to relent until he heard

everything he wanted to hear, squeezing her malleable flesh again.

"Marc, master," she faltered.

Her buttocks were so sensitive, her sheath empty and aching for release. When he shifted his hand to trace his fingers down her crack with a light rasping over her anus and then her slit before returning to fondle her cheeks, a groan of frustration slipped past her compressed lips. Unable to stop herself, she ground against his hard muscled thigh, seeking relief from the consuming ache he had built. She'd never considered her butt an erogenous zone, never imagined her buttocks could be so responsive. She'd never experienced arousal to this degree just from having her ass played with, but *oh, God*, it felt so good.

Marc watched with satisfaction as she fought against the arousal he induced from caressing her ass and the light touches on her anus and pussy. It was a battle he determined she would lose. He had always been an ass man, and she had a world class one he knew he'd never tire of fondling. As eager as he was to smack those delectable globes, he was just as eager to see if he could get her to orgasm by just playing with her.

He continued alternating soft strokes with hard kneading, followed by a light graze from her anus down her seeping slit, gliding over her protruding, swollen clit before taking a casual trail back up her crack and then resuming fondling her buttocks. When her hips ground against his thigh then lifted for more caresses in a rapid rhythm, he knew he had her.

Cassie's whole backside and pussy were aflame with so much sensation, her entire body quivered with it. With total disbelief, she began shaking with the beginning tremors of an orgasm then cried out in shocked ecstasy as it burst in a kaleidoscope of color upon her. Not caring how lewd she must look gyrating her naked butt over his lap, lifting up and down between his thigh and his hand, she rode out the pleasure until she lay like a limp noodle over his thighs in sated bliss.

The first slap landed with a resounding crack in the center of both her cheeks, shocking her out of her pleasant afterglow euphoria.

"Say, 'Thank you, master,' after each one."

Delivered in a harsh voice, his order was at odds with the way he softly rubbed the burning mark on her butt. "Thank you, master." She never considered defying his order as she braced for the next smack, surprised at how easily those three words came out of her mouth.

His next swat landed on her right buttock with as much force as the first. Sinking her teeth into her lip, she embraced with the familiar pleasure/pain that never failed to arouse her. He wasn't starting soft and working up to harder strokes as usual, yet she welcomed each swat with pleasure, greeted each with a lift of her hips and thanked him for each on a gasp of pain that seeped into renewed pleasure, the tiny tremors still gripping her vagina increasing with each slap.

Watching her come apart over his lap had increased his own lust tenfold. Marc landed two more strokes then fingered her sheath, found her soaking, her engorged clit hard and swollen, her thighs trembling with her need. Pulling away from her tempting pussy, he swatted her ass again, loving the way her voice caught as she thanked him.

"Good girl, darlin'. I love your ass, how it looks now, all red and quivering, hot under my hand." He gave her another hard blow in the middle of her cheeks then moved to her thighs to apply a few lighter smacks before grazing her slit and inching his way up her crack to caress her small tight hole.

She released a low, tortured groan when he tantalized the sensitive nerve endings around her anus and then slipped his finger inside, leaving him in no doubt about her acceptance. With a few shallow thrusts, he prepared her for further stimulation. "I'm going to fuck this ass soon, but today, I have a special treat for you."

Cassie missed his finger when he removed it and now she had to contend with having both orifices begging for attention. "Sir?" she questioned when she felt the slow push of a well lubed object into her anus.

"Don't worry, you'll like this," he assured her. "Deep breath now."

On her inhale, the dildo slipped all the way in, filling her deeper and stretching her wider than any of the plugs she had used. Marc caressed her sore, tingling buttocks, and she imagined what she looked like with her butt bare and impaled, her cheeks red and her denuded labia glistening with her seeping juices. That mental picture set her to shaking with renewed arousal and wondering when he would put out this new fire he had started.

"Master, I need to come." She cringed at her desperation-laced tone but the need for more was far greater than her embarrassment.

"Oh, we're a long way from that."

His amused tone had her gritting her teeth, swearing in frustration. Her sharp cry echoed in the clearing when he landed a brutal swat right over the dildo.

"I heard that curse. Be patient and trust me to take care of you."

"But I want you to take care of me now," she whined, not caring if she sounded petulant.

"Cassie."

His low warning came with a stinging pinch to her reddened buttock. "*Ow!*"

"Come here." Helping her up, Marc settled her on his lap, pushed her shorts the rest of the way off then pulled her shirt over her head. The sunlight filtering through the trees splashed across her naked breasts, warming them for his lips. With one arm behind her back, he lifted her toward his mouth and latched onto a turgid peak, sucking deeply as he used his free hand to pull and roll her other nipple.

The dual stimulation had her gasping with the new pleasure/pain then groaning in frustration when he released her tormented buds all too soon. "What are you doing?" she asked as he leaned down and rummaged through his backpack.

"Getting another toy for you." Marc found what he was searching for, thankful he had taken these toys out of their packages before leaving the lodge.

"What's that?"

She watched as he slipped the two loops over her ankles and up to her crotch. Attached in the middle of the loops was a soft, rectangular stimulator he nestled between her folds, right next to her puffy clit.

"You've never used a butterfly?"

"No." But she had heard of them. Master Greg had wanted to use toys, but she had declined, just one of the things she denied him that had displeased him. Making sure the bands stretched tight enough over her hips to hold the little piece in place, he lifted her off his lap, smiling when she wobbled a little.

"What's wrong, darlin'?"

"Nothing," she denied, narrowing her eyes at him. With her ass stretched around the dildo and her sensitive clit teased by the press of the small rubber vibrator, her overly charged senses hummed with arousal, her orgasm having done little to curb her desire.

Taking her hand, he led her to a large tree, reached up and pulled down a chain with two attached cuffs. Lifting her hands, he wrapped the cuffs around her wrists with quick efficiency she remembered all too well, not giving her a chance to think before cupping her face in his wide palms and tipping her head up to his. His lips came down on hers in hard possession, kissing the tenseness from the taut stretch of her body as she leaned into him with a moan of surrender.

"Remember, use your safeword if you need to."

Liquid heat filled her when she tested her bonds with a sharp tug, eliciting a drawing need that was almost overwhelming. "Yes, sir."

With a nod and a smile, he went back to his bag and retrieved two more items. Seeing the blindfold and flogger, a frisson of fear accompanied the anticipation coursing through her overstimulated body. She shut her mind against the horrid memory of her last session with Master Greg that had ended with such excruciating pain. Master Marc was not Master Greg and a flogger wasn't a thin, wieldy cane.

"Do you trust me, Cassie?"

Looking into his serious eyes, she knew she did. It was only one reason she had risked everything to return to him. She had trusted him two years ago until she made the grave mistake of looking upon his actions as a betrayal. "Yes, yes, Marc, I do." She omitted his title on purpose, letting him know she trusted him as a master but also as her friend and lover.

Marc kissed her brow. "Thank you. Today is for you." Covering her eyes with the soft blindfold, he added, "All I want you to do is feel."

He lowered his hands to caress her face, her lips, before stroking in slow exploration down her neck, over her breasts, squeezing her waist, her buttocks, and then running his fingers over her mound and between her legs with a gliding touch. When she pushed her hips forward, she heard his low chuckle and felt him step back.

Cassie jerked with the first stroke of the flogger, not from pain but from pleasure. The leather strands softly kissed her buttocks, the light stings from each rawhide strip quickly gone. Moving up her back, then down and over her butt and thighs, he teased her with a litany of soft, tantalizing strikes. Her breathing increased as anticipation rose along with the strength behind the strokes. Just as she got into the rhythm, let herself sway with each burning lash, he stopped, her curse escaping on a whimper.

"Master?"

"Oh, I like that, how my title fell so naturally from your lips," Marc whispered in her ear from behind her. Reaching down, he flicked the vibrator in her ass and then the remote for the butterfly in his pocket. He had both settings set on low, but by her flushed face and soft moan, it was enough for now.

Swaying in her restraints to the rhythm of tiny pulses in her rectum and against her clit, her need for more ratcheted up with each burning lash. Her back, buttocks, and thighs tingled where the flogger struck her. The soft breeze caressed her skin and the warm, soothing touch of sunlight splashing her body lulled her into lethargy. She heard the twitter of birds singing, the rustle of leaves from the light breeze and Marc stepping back. When he struck this time, the thin leather strands landed with a much sharper sting, the sudden blistering pain rousing her with a yelp and jerk, tantalizing enough to have her swaying back for more. He struck fast and steady this time around, harder than before but not the unbearable strikes Master Greg gave her with a cane before being stopped by another dom after ignoring her safeword. She shoved that memory aside, refusing to let it intrude or mar this time with Marc.

Moving with slow, methodical expertise between her thighs and back, taking extra time to torment the globes of her butt, he had her writhing in her bonds, unsure whether she wanted to escape the brutal strikes or embrace them. As they intensified, so did her excitement, answering her own question. When he moved in front of her and switched back to light strokes against her sensitive breasts, her tormented cry startled even her.

Slight burning streaked across the fleshy mounds of her breasts with each carefully orchestrated snap of leather, the sharp nip on her nipple from the end of one strand sending her lust careening toward a cliff from which there would be no stopping the tumble over. Soft caresses of striking rawhide traversed down her stomach before the unexpected sharp blow on the tender, bare skin of her labia threw her headlong over that cliff, screaming in pleasure all the way down. Shaking, she rocked with the explosive climax as the intense sensations drove the breath from her body, then continued, alternating hard and soft strokes from the flogger along with the vibrations in her rectum and against her clit egging her on. Soon she couldn't tell when one climax ended and another began, she just went with the flow, drowning in pleasure and awash in sensation.

Marc's face swam into view when he removed the blindfold. Blinking, she took a moment to come to her senses as he lowered her arms and cuddled her against his hard body. The rapid beat of his heart beneath her ear matched her own frantic rhythm, the hard cock pressing against her stomach proof it wasn't because of a climax, or two, but because of how much he needed to take her.

"You look beautiful with your pink striped skin and shining eyes."

His compliment went straight to her unguarded heart, rendering her speechless. Before he noticed, she pulled back and released his cock, taking him in a tight grip, the seductive smile creasing his lean cheeks encouraging her to explore further. Fisting him with one hand, she cupped his balls with the other, rolling them in her palm. The stark hunger reflected in his penetrating eyes was more than she could stand, but before she could drop to her knees to take him in her mouth, he cursed, grabbed her arms, and turned her back toward the log.

"Bend over." Marc winced with the way his harsh tone revealed his urgent need to get inside her. Witnessing her unbridled reaction to the flogging, the way her head arched back, sending her long red-gold hair flowing around her shoulders, her buttocks clenching around the vibrator and her hips thrusting with the pleasure, damn near made him come in his jeans. Her effect on him proved to be more than he ever envisioned, solidifying his growing feelings.

Trying not to think of anything but the moment, he sheathed himself in a condom, shoved her legs further apart, grabbed her hips, and thrust into her wet heat. Finding the remote to the butterfly, he flicked it on high and fucked her the way he had fantasized, rough and hard.

Cassie swallowed her disappointment when she felt his latex-covered cock. After allowing him to restrain and blindfold her in the middle of the wilderness, giving him her explicit trust with her safety and well-being, he still didn't trust her enough to believe in her precautions. She longed to feel his bare cock filling her, teasing her walls with the hard ridges of his length, but he apparently wasn't ready to take that step. His forceful shove drew a grunt from her pent-up breath and, condom or no, her sheath folded around him and clasped him in a tight grip of welcome and need.

Then the small pad nestled against her clit came on full force, stimulating her still sensitive nub with hard pulses, sending her straight into another orgasm. Her hands slipped off the log as the blood rushed to her head with no warning. Sliding an arm around her waist, he held her up as he pumped a few more times into her tight core before she felt him erupt inside her, his shout reverberating across the mountain top along with her cries.

· · · · · · ·

To Cassie's relief, they made the hike back down to the lodge much faster and easier. She ached all over from the unaccustomed exercise. The hiking left her legs tired and weak and the multiple orgasms and vigorous fucking left her feeling raw and vulnerable. She knew what a demanding lover he could be, but now she had to come to terms with knowing her heart was involved, adding to the angst of her battered feelings. Two years ago there had only been the potential of falling in love with her dom; now she faced the reality. It took an eye-opening, shattering experience with another dom to force her to see the truth; she had fallen fast and hard for Marc in the beginning and those feelings hadn't changed, only grown more intense.

And now she knew she wanted him and all he offered. But other than protecting her from an anonymous stalker and enjoying sex with her, he gave no hint how he felt about her.

"You're too quiet," Marc commented as they approached the lodge, his hand wrapped around hers. He wondered if he had pushed too hard again, if she was contemplating running and what he would do if she did.

She smiled up at him, trying to ease the worry on his face. He didn't trust her, and maybe he had good reason not to. After that last disastrous night together in the Omaha club, it still surprised her he had greeted her as openly as he had and wanted to protect her. She often regretted cutting off their communication after that following week as much as she regretted running from him.

"I'm tired and know I'm going to be sore tomorrow. All that hiking and outdoor activity has my body aching already."

"I forgot you're not accustomed to such long hikes. Why don't you go soak in the hot tub around back. I'll join you after I help Jack get dinner started."

"You have a hot tub? That sounds wonderful," she all but moaned. Shoving past regrets aside, she gave him a swift kiss before making her way around the lodge to the back, looking forward to the warm jets of water pulsing against her sore muscles.

CHAPTER EIGHT

Cassie came to an abrupt halt when she spotted Morgan lounging naked in the hot tub, but her automatic smile of welcome got her feet moving again. "I don't want to disturb you, but that looks too enticing to pass up."

"Drop your clothes and get in," Morgan invited. "I always need a good soak after a hike with Jack." Her eyes twinkled. "Did you enjoy your outing?"

She tried hard not to blush, but knew she failed when Morgan laughed. "Okay, I think I could get used to outdoor sex," she admitted. Wasting no time, she shed her clothes and eased into the heated, swirling water with a sigh of pure bliss as she sank down. "*Aaah*, this feels wonderful." Submerging up to her shoulders and leaning her head back against the cushioned edge, she closed her eyes and let the steam work its magic.

"Yeah, me too. The winters here are long, but trust me, those two can find inventive ways to keep you warm outdoors."

Morgan relayed the details of her first outdoor spanking in the frigid temperatures and how Jack had cooled her burning ass with snow. The scene she conjured up had Cassie sinking even deeper into the hot, bubbly water.

"Oh, *ow*, that doesn't sound pleasant."

"You wouldn't think, would you? I admit it did nothing to cool my ardor."

Closing her eyes, she let her mind float along with her body, but she couldn't stop from wondering just how involved Marc was with Jack and Morgan. Opening her eyes again, she glanced over at her new friend and had to swallow her jealousy. Morgan's full figure and sparkling topaz eyes would attract any man. Even though Morgan was only an inch or two taller than her, Cassie felt like a short stick next to the other woman.

Morgan glanced at her, her smile soft and encouraging. "Relax. Marc doesn't want me, not the way he wants you."

"How do you know what I'm thinking?" Her irritation over her transparency colored her tone. If Morgan could see the depth of her need for Marc, could he?

"It's written all over your face, mostly when you're looking at him. Look, I won't lie, Marc has joined us a few times. But the only thing I've ever done with him is given him a blowjob. When they get possessive, the sharing only goes so far."

"But he's spanked you?" she asked, relieved the three of them didn't indulge in sex together that often.

"Oh, sure, several times." She frowned as she added in a darker tone, "There was even one time Jack gave him permission to use his belt on me. I didn't sit down for two days!"

Cassie laughed at her feigned look of outrage. "What'd you do?"

Morgan's frown turned into a saucy, mischievous grin. "I got caught spying on two of our more inventive guests in the woods."

"What's wrong with watching? There were plenty of people watching you on your birthday." The heat surrounding her seeped into her aching, overused muscles, relaxing her and making it easier for her to sit naked with another woman for the first time and converse as if she didn't feel self-conscious.

"I wasn't just watching. I got so turned on I did something about it, and Jack has this ridiculous, strict rule I can't masturbate without his permission and giving him a chance to watch. It really gets him going when I get myself off." Morgan rolled her eyes but was smiling.

"That seems unfair." She had masturbated a lot in the past months, always to memories of her few nights with Marc. "I wonder how Marc feels about it. I don't think I'd like it if he insisted I get his permission to touch myself. When the mood strikes, who wants to wait to seek permission?"

"Oh, I agree a hundred percent. So, want to see what he would do?"

"You mean now?" She looked around to see if he lurked somewhere, but didn't see him or anyone else.

"Don't look up, but both Marc and Jack have been watching us from upstairs. They have a good view from the windows in the great room. What do you say we give them a show?"

The idea sent arousal swirling through her overheated system, warming her from the inside as much as the hot tub warmed her skin. The intensity of her reaction surprised her, coming so soon after she came like a firecracker a short while ago. Knowing both men watched added to her excitement as did the mental picture of Marc applying his belt to Morgan's butt. "It seems Marc's belt wasn't much of a deterrent for you."

Morgan returned Cassie's knowing grin. "Not much, no."

"Well," she said, raising her hands to her breasts to cup them. "I *am* feeling relaxed," she pulled her nipples, "and warm," she kneaded the soft mounds.

"Mmm, me too," Morgan agreed and copied her by cupping her own breasts and pinching her nipples. "A nice, long orgasm would be welcome right about now."

"Son of a bitch," Marc muttered, watching Cassie cup her breasts and toy with her pouty nipples until they became rigid. They couldn't hear what the women were saying, but their actions spoke loud and clear. He turned accusing eyes on Jack as if it was his fault the two were egging them on. "Morgan has a short memory."

"Maybe it was Cassie's idea," Jack replied, knowing full well it wasn't. His little minx was up to her pranks again. "Okay," he conceded when Marc raised an eyebrow in silence. "We may as well enjoy their little game before we go down there and remind them who's boss."

"Good idea." Looking down again, Marc's mouth watered at the sight of Cassie leaning her head back with her eyes closed, her teeth nibbling on her lower lip as she tortured her nipples into even tighter, redder peaks. His cock stiffened and if he didn't get himself under control he risked permanent zipper indentations in his flesh. When she inched her right hand down her waist, under the water to cup her sweet pussy, he gave up on any hope of getting himself under control.

Luckily for them, the girls had slid away from the jets and the men had a clear view where their hands traveled. With her legs spread, Cassie slid two fingers into her sheath, arching into the caress. Her hips continued to lift toward her marauding hand, those gyrations responsible for the breakout of light perspiration on his skin. When she smiled over at Morgan, said something that sent them scooting back over to the jets, he knew his favorite appendage was in trouble if they didn't get down there soon.

"She won't be able to sit down for a week," Jack growled, watching his fiancée coming apart under the powerful jets pummeling against her pussy.

"I don't think Cassie knows how much more my hand will hurt against her wet ass." Marc lowered his zipper inch by slow inch as Cassie spread her labia in front of a fast, pulsating jet then threw her head back and came with a loud wail. With his hand wrapped around his cock, he turned toward the back stairs leading to the hot tub and garden area, Jack following close behind him.

• • • • • • •

Cassie shuddered as the last tremors from her climax settled down. She had never come that hard from masturbating before and she could only attribute its intensity to her audience. Floating in a lazy glide away from the jet, she turned back around in time to catch Morgan's "Oh, shit" and worried look.

Striding toward them, hard cocks in tight fists, Marc and Jack looked pissed.

"Hi, master."

Morgan greeted Jack with her eyes on his dick, her breath short from her explosive orgasm, and Cassie had to admire her friend's bravado, not that she believed Jack would harm her. The glint in his eyes spoke volumes about how much he cared.

"Why are you out of breath, princess?" Jack asked in a silky tone. "I don't recall giving you permission to touch yourself let alone to come."

"If you get naked and join me, I'll show you how sorry I am."

Her look said otherwise, then Marc stripped and stepped down into the hot tub, snagging Cassie's attention, the erotic sight of him fisting his erection sending a heated flush up her neck to cover her face.

"Take care of your sub, Jack. I'll deal with mine."

"You never said I couldn't masturbate, master," she told him as he stood thigh deep in the water, his cock an enticing lure for her mouth.

"But I'm sure Morgan told you the rules."

Grabbing her hair at her nape, he urged her forward. There were no thoughts of refusal as he pushed his cock into her eager mouth.

"How well you suck me off will determine how hard I spank you when you're done."

Cassie closed her lips around his smooth crown, her buttocks clenching in both dread and anticipation at the mention of another spanking on the tender skin where he flogged her. How the two combined could have her nipples pebbling and her vagina spasming was beyond her. Wrapping her arms around his hips, she clutched his firm ass and urged him closer, his cock deeper. Alternating suckling him with hard pulls with teasing strokes over his ridged thickness, she savored the taste of him, the heavy feel of him in her mouth.

He held her head with a tight grip of her hair, controlling her movements and adding to her growing excitement. Using both tongue and lips, she explored his plum-shaped head, dipped into the seeping slit then caressed the softer underside with slow strokes. His low groans gave her courage, the hold of her hair kept her from straying from where he craved her most, the tight clench of his buttocks in her hands told her she was doing it right. Recalling a trick she had read about, she ran a finger down his crack, made a light graze over his anus then moved down to the sensitive spot between his butt and his balls. When he spread his legs with a curse, she knew she'd hit the right spot. Trading his cheeks for his balls, she worked his cock until he quickened in her mouth. Peeking sideways at the other couple, she noted Jack's flushed face and found it exciting to know they'd ejaculate almost simultaneously.

Marc closed his eyes, rocking into her mouth, her soft hands on his balls, his perineum and his anus driving him crazy. When he got his sanity back he'd have to ask her where she learned about that spot. Then again, looking down into her pleasure-filled blue eyes, her cheeks bulging with his cock, maybe he didn't want to know.

"Get ready, darlin'," was all the warning he gave her before his climax erupted in a tidal wave of sensation.

Groaning, he kept a tight hold of his cock at the base so he didn't choke her, but the sight of her mouth and throat working to bring him such pleasure while swallowing every drop of his come came close to undoing him.

Jack shouted his release as Marc slowed his thrusts. Cassie continued to suckle him, cleaning every inch of his cock and drawing out every drop of come, which proved to be as pleasurable as her blowjob. When he leaned down and kissed her, he tasted himself on her tongue. When he held her face up, her tight grip on his wrists stated louder than words she didn't mind his taste.

"Very good, Cassie," he praised her against her swollen lips. "Now, kneel on the seat and bend over the back of the tub."

Her heart tripping with excitement, she replied, "Yes, sir," without qualm. Leaning her elbows on the padded back of the tub, she lowered her head waiting for the first blow to land. Why did she crave this with such longing? She had gone months without feeling a man's hand striking her ass, without the pain and humiliation adding to her pleasure. And now, after just a few days under Marc's rule again, she couldn't imagine going without it.

The first smack showed her what a difference wet skin could make. He whacked her hard, the blistering sting going straight south to her sheath. Morgan's cry accompanied hers as the rhythmic sound of slapping flesh resonated throughout the secluded yard. Another swat landed on her other cheek with blossoming pain, but before pleasure could blossom from it, he was smacking her again, a steady litany of slaps.

Looking over at Morgan, she grunted with the next smack then growled at her new friend, "You didn't warn me it hurts more when wet."

"Oops, sorry," Morgan quipped right before crying out over a particularly hard smack.

"Quiet, both of you," Jack snapped.

Marc grinned when Cassie shuddered then laid her head

down to accept her spanking. Damn, but he loved that pose of acceptance. Bent over with her ass on prominent display, nicely rounded and now an enticing deep red, he thought he had never seen such a delectable sight. Smacking her again right in the middle of those plump cheeks sent his cock to twitching with renewed interest. Her whimpers added to his pleasure and he knew the wetness coating those swollen pussy lips didn't come from the water. Fisting his cock, he delivered several more hard blows before reaching over and grabbing a condom from his jeans pocket. Wasting no time covering himself, he clasped her hips and thrust into her, burying himself balls deep with one deep stroke.

The clearing now resonated with the sounds of coupling, of flesh slapping flesh, of grunts and groans as the four of them approached climax. The evening air had cooled, but Cassie felt feverish as Marc's cock reamed her over and over, her buttocks pulsing, burning hot, her sheath full and stretched. When he reached in front of her and pinched her clit, she buried her head again, muffling her scream. Ecstasy enveloped her as she thrust back against him while bearing down against his fingers as he milked her clit with tight pulls.

Sobbing, she took everything he gave her and prayed there would be something left of her when he finished because she knew she wanted to be more to him than just another submissive woman. She had returned to him to not only earn his trust again, but to gain his love.

"He's driving me crazy!" Cassie complained to Michelle a few days later. "If he's not dogging my every move between here and the lodge, then he has Scott or one of his guys stopping in here every hour. People will wonder what's going on if they don't lighten up."

"I think it's sweet," Michelle said as she arranged fresh baked cookies in the display case.

"Sweet? It's nerve-racking." She counted out the receipts for the past week and would have been pleased if not for the constant, irksome interruptions. Between the frequent visits from the sheriff or his people and Marc's constant phone calls, she couldn't get anything done. To make matters worse, she felt so guilty about taking up so much of the deputies' time she insisted they pick something from the case to take with them when they left, which encouraged them to stop in more often.

It had been sheer bad luck when Scott stepped inside her bakery just as she opened another plain white envelope yesterday and snatched it from her. That message had been short, too short as all the cutup newspaper letters spelled was one word: *Soon*. Okay, so she had been a little shaken, but their response was over the top.

"I'd love it if a guy cared about me so much that his worry would make him so overprotective."

Cassie smiled at the younger girl. At nineteen, her naivety could be excused. She'd give anything to have just met Marc, to have this time with him untarnished by the stupid mistakes from their past. If it wasn't for the wariness and mistrust she caught on his face when he didn't think she saw him, she could almost believe he cared as much if not more than he had two years ago. He still wanted her though, as much it seemed as he had back then. For now, she'd have to settle for that and hope in time his feelings would grow as deep as hers seemed to have always been.

"He's just looking out for me. Don't read any more into it than that."

Michelle rolled her eyes. "I've seen the way he looks at you. Open your eyes, Cassie, you might see more that way."

Wondering if Michelle had a point made it difficult for her to keep her mind on task the rest of the afternoon. Could he care for her a little? Vacillating between hope and denial took her mind off that last message. She had fallen fast and hard for him when they first met, so fast and so hard she had been devastated when she entered the club on that third night and learned he planned on sharing her with Jack. At the time, shock led her to believe he betrayed her, but now, the memory just made her sad.

Cassie spotted him right away. She didn't see the other newbies she'd befriended, or the doms they were paired with for their last night, only him. Seeing him leaning on the polished bar top, his pose elegant, his look watchful, had her palms sweating, set her heart to pounding. He stood next to his friend, Jack, and even though he was an inch or two shorter than Jack, he still stood taller than others around him and towered over her. His size made her feel small and when he had that hard body wrapped around her, she felt cherished and safe. Wiping her clammy palms down her skirt, she wondered what he had planned for tonight. Two weeks ago she could never have imagined herself having sex in public with a guy she had only known two days, but she had and she loved it and was very much afraid she loved him. He was older, more experienced and worldly than her, making her wonder what he saw in her, why he wanted her. Then he spotted her, gave her that slow smile responsible for curling her toes as he strode with purpose toward her and she forgot about her misgivings.

"Hi." She returned his smile then melted when he pulled her to him and kissed her without a word. Groaning, Cassie sank into the kiss, loving how his lips took command of hers the same way his body did. When he drew her arms behind her and clasped her wrists in a tight grip, she shivered with longing, eager now to feel his hard cock taking her again. She didn't care where or how, so long as it was soon.

"Hi yourself," he responded when he lifted his mouth from hers, their lips so close her breath mingled with his. "Let's sit over here."

Her hand clasped in his, she followed him to an empty sofa in a quiet, secluded corner where he wasted no time in baring her breasts.

"Did you wear this to make it easy for me?" he asked as she leaned into him.

"Yes." Breathless, Cassie arched into his hands, excitement replacing modesty as he tortured her nipples with hard pinches followed by the soothing touch of his lips and stroke of his tongue. "I've thought of nothing but you lately."

Marc lifted his head and his green eyes bored into hers. "That's good because I've thought of nothing but you too. Cassie, I don't want this, us, to end after tonight."

"But you live in Colorado." Her pleasure at hearing he wanted more time with her dimmed with the reality of their situation. "Long-

distance relationships rarely work out."

"We'll make it work," he insisted. "I work for myself. I can arrange to come here, at least for a few days, about once a month. You can come to Colorado and stay at our lodge during semester breaks from teaching. It won't cost you anything. I'll send you a plane ticket. Do you teach in the summer?"

His hands and mouth stayed busy on her breasts as he pled his case, making it difficult to concentrate. Her happy places throbbed from his attention, ached for more. Rubbing the inflamed ache between her legs against his prominent erection, she whimpered with escalating need. "Just tutoring."

"We'll work it out. Tell me you want to try as much as I do. That's all I ask."

"Yes, yes, of course I do." Her thighs fell open when he inched her skirt up. "Oh, God," she moaned as he deftly slid her thong off and cupped her aching sheath.

"You're wet, darlin'. Even your pretty curls are damp. Tell me you don't get this wet for just any guy," he demanded.

"I don't," she gasped as he entered her with two fingers. "I honestly don't. This isn't like me." Arching into his hand, she laid her head back against his arm and gloried in the easy way he could arouse her, oblivious to the sights and sounds around them.

He drove her crazy tormenting her, his fingers filling her, exploring every inch of her vagina while rasping his thumb over her clit. He kept her body strung taut on a low simmer, never allowing her to boil over. Frustration and need had her perspiring, cursing, and pleading as she begged him for release.

"Please, please, master. More, I need more."

"She begs so nice."

Cassie's eyes flew open to see Jack sitting on the chair opposite them, his erection a blatant bulge in his slacks, his dark eyes warm and caressing as he looked at her bent, splayed legs and Marc's hand between them. With her skirt pulled to her waist and her top lowered, she lay bared and exposed.

Marc tightened his arm around her when she attempted to cover herself. "Stay still."

His deep voice and the implacable look on his face had her obeying without thought. Then he smiled, the approval lighting his eyes forcing her to bite her lip to keep from blurting out she loved him.

"Good girl. Let me show Jack how pretty you look as you come apart, begging for more, darlin'."

He took her mouth in a hard kiss, finger fucking her with deep, hard strokes. This time when he pressed his thumb on her clit, he didn't let up on the pressure. His mouth left hers and returned to her breasts, the arm behind her back holding her up to him. She had no defense from the ruthless, dual stimulation, her orgasm bursting with a kaleidoscope of colors, her hips grinding against his hand as he pumped into her with furious strokes. Her body shook as sensation after sensation swamped her, leaving her shaken and limp on his lap, uncaring she still lay sprawled in lewd display. She relished his softer strokes now, the soothing caresses meant to calm her rioting emotions.

As she tried to calm her labored breathing, he whispered in her ear, "Cassie, have you ever fantasized about having two men?"

"What?" Still reeling from her explosive climax, she grappled a moment to grasp his words.

"Just think, darlin'. Four hands, two lips, two cocks, all working to please you."

Cassie jerked away from him, shaking as if doused in cold water, shock and betrayal leaving her shattered. "You want to share me? With him?" She glanced at Jack and saw the truth in his face.

"I want to please you, we both do. I promise…"

Jumping off his lap, she wasted no time straightening her clothes, her throat clogged with shame, shame she hadn't felt the past few nights until this moment. Casting a frantic look around, she spotted her thong at the end of the sofa and snatched it up. Marc had risen and now tried to take her arm. Jerking back, she cried out in a voice hoarse with pain and accusation, "Don't touch me! I thought… I thought…" Tears choked her as she looked at him and saw not the man she thought she loved but the one who cared so little for her he would not only allow but abet another man touching her, fucking her. "I thought you cared."

"I do, damn it. Cassie, wait. Let's talk, don't run off…"

"I don't want to talk. Coming here was a mistake, one I won't make again. Men like you want more, expect more, than I'm willing to give."

"Wait," he barked in his dom's voice, the one that brooked no argument and demanded instant obedience. The one that, until this moment, sent ripples of pleasure down her spine.

"Cherry. There, I said my safeword and we're through, I'm through." Turning, she fled through the club with blinding tears, her heart breaking, and she never looked back.

Cassie could recall that night with a clearer head now, maybe because she wasn't blinded by infatuation and deeply ingrained moral convictions. Maturity forced her to be honest with herself, first regarding her stagnant relationship with Rick, and second with what she really wanted when it came to sex and a relationship. Those few nights with Master Greg confirmed she got off on domination; his betrayal had shown Marc's actions in a whole new light and her reunion with Marc confirmed it was him and only him she wanted to submit body and soul to. It took her awhile, months in fact, to admit one reason she climaxed so hard that night under his hand was because of Jack's presence. She remembered thinking it a big turn-on that he got hard watching her, that he was fantasizing about fucking her, that he might want her. But the shock of Marc's plan had obliterated everything but the sense of betrayal. Watching Morgan with two men, the way they catered to her, their every touch designed to heighten her pleasure, had been an aphrodisiac in itself. And seeing the possessive way Jack looked at Morgan afterward and since had her aching for the same look from Marc.

The door chiming claimed her attention and with a start she realized it was almost closing time. She put away the last few items and went out to greet Marc with less frustration than when he dropped her off. If Michelle was right and his overprotectiveness stemmed from his growing feelings for her, she would try to be more patient.

CHAPTER NINE

It pleased Marc when Cassie became more acceptable of his protection, but he wouldn't have minded using her rubber spatula on her again if she hadn't. When he picked her up earlier, she didn't start in on how ridiculous it was for him to make two trips to town each day even after another threatening note arrived. When it concerned her safety, he wasn't willing to take any chances. The thought of someone hurting her made him see red, and there would be no stopping him from seeking justice if it came to that.

A decision would have to be made soon concerning their relationship. Right now they were together because of circumstances. If he were honest with himself, he would admit he had been losing the battle to stay away from her when Scott contacted him about the first note she received. He also knew no one could coerce him into doing anything he didn't want to do, including having sex, no matter how much he wanted it. Cassie, he knew, thought she was only in his bed because she refused to come stay at the lodge any other way. He let her think that, not yet ready to admit to her how much he still wanted her, how her bravery and determination to seek him out again had torn down all his defenses. The fear she would disappear from his life a second time still plagued him, making it difficult for him to ease her mind just yet or lower his guard all the way. But he was getting closer to accepting her back into his life, of putting the past behind him.

"Everything ready?" Jack asked, pulling Marc out of his thoughts.

Looking around the club room, he nodded his head. "Yeah. Only about ten of the group checked in today. You said about twelve more will be here for the weekend?"

"Yes, they're all checking in after three on Friday." Turning to head back upstairs, Jack asked, "Do you plan to scene with Cassie tonight?"

"She's had enough experience to know what to expect, so yes. It still irks me she sought another dom before coming here, but I can understand why she did it."

"You're not worried about rushing her?"

Jack knew him well and Marc had confided in him about his remorse over moving too fast with Cassie the last time, how the way she freaked out and the betrayed look in her blue eyes preyed on him.

"A little, but this time is different. She's older, more experienced, and nothing we do or she sees will be a surprise. This time she'll have no excuse to bolt, at least not out of fear of betrayal."

"So, you have no plans to share her?"

There was no way he could suppress the need to see her pleasured by two men. She was so sexy and so open with her sexuality now that just thinking of the ways he and another man could bring her pleasure made him hard. "I didn't say that, but this time she'll at least have a forewarning."

As they entered their loft they heard giggling coming from the kitchen where the girls were finishing the dinner dishes. "They get on well," Jack murmured, pleased Morgan had found a close friend.

"And they'll keep us on our toes if the hot tub incident is anything to go by," Marc returned with dry humor.

"That pleases you as much as it does me."

Cassie squealed in surprise when Marc's arms circled her from behind, startling her. "Sorry, darlin'. I thought you heard me come in."

She could tell from his tone he wasn't sorry at all. She and Morgan had been joking around and she hadn't noticed their return.

"Let me go, you big oaf." She smiled at him over her shoulder. "If you want me to join you downstairs I need to finish these dishes and take a shower." He made a show of sniffing her neck, making her laugh.

"Mmm, you smell good, like sugar and cinnamon."

"Exactly. I smell like a bakery and sweat," she returned, wrinkling her nose.

"You smell sweet and I happen to like sweet, but I'll let you go for now since I want nothing to ruin my plans for you tonight."

"You're not going to tell me anything, are you?"

"No, but trust me, you'll enjoy yourself."

Turning in his arms, she looped her soapy hands around his neck. "I do, Marc. Trust you, that is. I want you to know that. I'm not that naïve newbie anymore who didn't know a good thing when I had it."

Marc kissed her, wanting to believe her. "Finish your chores, girl, then meet me downstairs. I have to get back down there to greet our guests. I put one of my shirts on the bed. Wear that and nothing else."

She watched him leave, well aware he hadn't responded to her statement.

"I wore nothing but Jack's shirt the first week I was here. Why does wearing a guy's shirt feel more intimate, sexier than a sheer nightie he gave you?"

From Morgan's sympathetic look, Cassie knew she hadn't concealed her worry over his lack of a response. "Maybe because the last place it had been was next to their skin, the same place we want to be."

"I hadn't thought of that, but I think you're onto

something there. Let's go get ready and see what our guys have planned for us tonight."

• • • • • • •

An hour later, she followed Morgan downstairs, the tantalizing brush of Marc's silk shirt against her nipples and bare butt heightening her already overwrought senses. It smelled like him, masculine and warm, and made her feel closer to him. The loud beat of classic rock didn't disguise the sounds of play already in progress when they reached the door to the clubroom. She relaxed when she saw just a small group gathered for tonight. The fewer people, the less distraction for her and the more she could concentrate on pleasing Marc. She remembered him telling her the first night she met him she would know she was truly submissive when she derived her deepest desire from pleasing him. She knew now what he meant.

"Do you know everyone?" she asked Morgan as they made their way to the bar where Jack waved them over.

"I recognize most of them, but I'm awful with names. It's easier to just smile and say 'How are you?'"

Cassie moved to hop on a barstool when hard hands grabbed her waist and boosted her up. "There you go, darlin'," Marc said, leaning a muscled arm on the bar, a small smile tugging at his lips.

Dressed in tight jeans and body-sculpting black tee shirt with the lodge's logo in the corner, he looked at her out of assessing green eyes.

"You look good in my shirt."

He caressed her bare thigh where the shirt had ridden up and Cassie had trouble keeping from spreading her legs open in invitation as her core moistened. *Talk about easy and eager*, she thought with a rueful sigh. "Thank you, Master Marc."

"I like how easily my title now falls from those pretty lips." As he grasped her hair, a thrill shot up her spine when he held her still for a deep, wet kiss that set her body to quivering with anticipation. "And I like how those lips feel under mine."

"Cassie, what can I get you?" Jack interrupted, grinning at her dazed expression. "Shit, Marc. All you did was kiss her. I can't wait to see her face after you've had her over the spanking bench for a while."

The shocked arousal filling her blue eyes drew a chuckle from both men. "Bring her a rum and Coke, Jack, and make it strong. She will need it."

Fifteen minutes later, he had the shirt gaping open and the strong drink had kicked in, loosening her body and warming her from the inside. Or maybe she should attribute the pleasant feeling to how Marc's hands were all over her bared breasts. Turning on the stool to face him, she shivered from the hard pinch and taut pull of both nipples.

"You like that little bite of pain, don't you?"

He didn't lift his eyes from her nipples, alternating between rolling them between his fingers and pinching. By the time he released them, the throbbing nubs were cherry red.

"Yes," she breathed, ignoring the couple standing next to them visiting with Jack and Morgan.

"Your breasts are so pretty, so soft as they fill my hands. Except here."

Opening his fingers, he rubbed his palms against her sensitive nubs in a circular motion. Pushing against him, she bit her lip to keep from begging for more. He was the only one who could arouse her so fast, and to such a depth she ceased to think of anything except the pleasure they could give each other. When he slowly stroked his right hand down her waist and cupped her pussy, she thought she'd come right then. Grasping his wrist for leverage, she pushed against his palm, a silent plea for more.

"You've got my hand all wet, darlin'. Shame on you," he murmured, pressing his palm harder between her spread legs, catching her juices as they seeped out then rubbing over her plump, soft folds.

"It's your fault," she accused him, her face warming when Scott walked up to lean with casual negligence against the bar, a beer dangling from his hand as his gray eyes looked her over in slow perusal.

"She's very pretty, Marc."

"Stop," Marc snapped when she attempted to close the shirt over her nakedness. "I didn't give you permission to cover yourself."

Cassie dropped her hands and tried looking away from both men. It was one thing to have strangers walking by or standing near and conversing with others while he played with her and another to have a man she knew and saw every day standing right in front of her, watching as Marc continued fondling her breasts and bared labia. But as disconcerting as she found Scott's close presence, she couldn't stem the rush of arousal as Marc slid one finger inside her.

After swirling his finger in her pussy, he raised his eyes to her flushed face and brought that finger to his mouth, his grin smug when her warm face turned hot. "She's also very wet," he told Scott before sucking his finger clean.

Scott slapped Marc on the back, his smile wide and wicked. "Give the poor girl some consolation. She deserves it."

Cassie breathed a sigh of relief when the sheriff strolled away. "I do, you know."

"I decide what you deserve, and don't. And right now, I think I'd like to see that pretty ass displayed over the spanking bench. I want to hear you scream when you come after being paddled," he whispered in her ear as he lifted her off the stool and took her hand.

She attempted to close the flapping shirt with her free hand, but his growled "Leave it" stayed her hand and made her wonder if the man had eyes in the back of his head.

When they reached the hip-high padded bench, he slipped the shirt off her shoulders and urged her down. Legs straight, Cassie lay prone on the bench, uneasy with her vulnerable exposure as he spread her legs and cuffed her ankles in place. When his large, warm, callused hands slid up her calves and thighs, she relaxed somewhat and when he skimmed his lips over her buttocks followed by a slow lick from her anus to her seam, her body rippled with renewed desire and anticipation.

Rising, Marc braced himself over her back, enveloping her small, shaking body with his. "Easy, darlin'," he soothed. "You've done this before." He arranged her breasts on either side of the narrower end of the bench so they hung down like small ripe fruits ready to be plucked. "If my memory serves me correctly, you liked being taken this way." Grabbing her right wrist, he kissed her clenched fist then drew her arm down and attached the cuff before doing the same to her left. "There. Restrained, spread, and available. How do you feel?"

"Scared, excited, exposed. Did I mention excited?" Cassie replied without evasion, not sure which emotion gripped her the strongest. There weren't that many people in the club, fewer than twenty. Other than Marc, Jack, and Morgan, she only recognized Scott from town, which helped ease the last of her hesitation.

"I'm proud of you for being so honest. Let's see if I can take your mind off everything except me."

She shivered with cold when he moved away from her, then shuddered with expected heat as he lifted a paddle off the wall and stepped behind her. The first smack from the round leather paddle stung as much as she remembered, the fiery burn it left behind soothed with his light caress. "Sir, please…" She pushed back into his hand, glad he hadn't strapped her hips down, her cheek throbbing from the hard swat.

"I do love hearing you beg."

He smacked her other cheek, then caressed the burning spot before slapping her again, this one a little harder. The steady pattern of swat, caress, swat, caress he set up, alternating between buttocks, drew her in, took over her senses until all she was aware of was the building painful pleasure consuming her. Unable to control her own body, her hips greeted each stroke with a welcoming lift.

She yelped with the hard blow he delivered to the middle of her butt then sobbed in a plea for relief. "Master, please, I need to come." Her hot, swollen globes fed her arousal, had her desperate for the pleasure of an orgasm to douse the encompassing fire.

"Not yet, darlin'." Marc peppered her buttocks with a few softer strokes then ran his palm over the warm rosy flesh. "You look beautiful, all red and hot." He squeezed her right buttock, smiling when she whimpered and rubbed against his hand. "And down here," he moved his hand between her spread cheeks to cover her pussy, "all warm and wet and soft." He traced her damp folds first then took a light dip between them before shifting to caress then slip into her tight back hole.

Gasping as he sank two damp fingers into her anus, she closed her eyes against the onslaught of sensation spreading through her entire backside. The moisture trickling from her sheath as he stroked deep inside her mortified her, but not enough to keep from arching against him. Sinking her teeth into her lip, she embraced the pleasure/pain he induced. An embarrassing moan of regret slipped past her tight lips when he pulled out of her followed by a startled gasp with the feathery whisper of his lips moving over her buttocks. Adding tongue and teeth, he covered every inch of her abused buttocks before moving down her crack, tonguing her asshole then licking her pussy.

Lost in a roiling sea of pleasure, she could do nothing but lie there and hope she didn't drown in the waves washing over her. All his concentration focused on her pussy and butt; his mouth kissed, nipped, and licked every inch of her flesh while his fingers explored her vagina, her anus, and everywhere in between. He brought her to the brink of orgasm again and again only to pull back before she could go over until she lay sobbing in frustration. Then he covered her with his hard body again, reached down to cup her dangling breasts, his jean-covered cock pushing between her cheeks.

"There are several people watching us. And now, they're going to see me take your ass. That's something we didn't get around to doing last time." Marc wiped the tears of frustration from her cheek before pulling back.

In dire need of an orgasm, Cassie didn't care who watched. The thought of him taking her in that taboo orifice for the first time in front of an audience didn't lessen her desire in the least. Tomorrow she might be ashamed; tonight she would bask in his possession. When he spread her buttocks and lubed her anus with two fingers, she shuddered with longing, aching to feel him inside her.

"Breathe out as I push in. It'll make it easier."

She did as he instructed but it still burned when he pushed inside her. Her gasp turned to a low moan when he kneaded her sore buttocks, his deep, soothing voice helping her relax until the pain eased and pleasure took its place. His cock stretched her wide with his girth, but, much to her relief, he held back from going too deep, keeping his thrusts shallow.

Marc forced himself to go slow, take his time and allow her body to adjust to the feel of him invading a foreign place. As he kept to short dips, she rewarded his restraint in less time than he expected, lifting to accept each little plunge. Her pleas gave him the permission he'd been waiting for to pick up the pace.

"Does that feel good? Do you like having me in your ass?" He winced at his harsh tone, perspiration coating his skin as he tried to rein in his lust.

"Yes, master, oh, yes. More, please, more." Cassie wasn't sure what she pleaded for, what she needed, but she trusted him to know and take care of that need.

"That's what I wanted to hear." Without further ado, he set up a harder pace, withdrawing until only his cock head remained past her rim before shoving back in, his thrusts increasing in speed but not depth as her soft cries egged him on. Reaching under her, he rooted out her clit, gave it a pinch as he reamed her ass just a little deeper, a little harder. "Come for me. Come now."

Her scream rent the air as she splintered apart, the myriad sensations so encompassing her vision went black. Lost in a vortex of explosive pleasure, she barely heard Marc's shout but felt every jerk of his cock as he joined her in the shocking bliss.

Her body exhausted from her exertions, her mind befuddled with the lingering pleasure, it took a sound that sent unreasonable terror slicing through her to pull her back into full awareness of her surroundings. Coming from her left, the distinct whoosh of a thin cane whipping through air followed by the snap of it on bare skin then a screech of pain sent her spiraling back three months when she had been the unwilling recipient of that harsh instrument. Panic overruled common sense, fear of experiencing that excruciating pain again, and remembered shock over the man she trusted ignoring her safeword had her struggling in her bonds, her breathing labored as she wept in silence.

"Let me go, let me go. I need to get up," she mewled over and over, wincing when her wrists and ankles wrenched in the bonds.

"Cassie!" Marc moved fast, joined by Scott who stood nearby. Releasing her cuffs, he snapped again as she continued to thrash. "Stop! Cassie, baby, I'm right here. *Shit, shit, shit,* what the hell happened?" Lifting her, his heart damn near lodged in his throat; he folded his arms around her shaking body and refused to let go even though she kept pleading with him to do so. "No. You're safe, Cassie. I've got you," he murmured in her ear, his gut turning cold as ice as he struggled to figure out what had caused her to panic like that.

"Bring her to the bar, I'll get her a drink," Scott instructed in his no-nonsense tone.

Cradling her in his arms, he looked down into her wide eyes and breathed a sigh of relief as he strode across the room. "Are you with me?" Perching on a barstool, he tightened his arm around her as he reached for the glass Scott handed him. "Drink."

Cassie roused at the command in his voice and took a big gulp of the whiskey, relishing the fiery burn down her throat that brought her the rest of the way back to full awareness. She couldn't believe how fast she panicked over hearing those sounds again, how quickly they thrust her into the past or how vivid her recollection still was of something that occurred over three months ago and she thought she put behind her. The last she saw of Master Greg he had been hauled out of the club by two angry doms, Master Wade cuddling her to his side and insisting on driving her home. Other than a few welts that took several days to heal, she thought she had come away from that horrible experience with nothing but regret.

"Want to tell me what the hell that was all about?"

She winced at his harsh tone and the underlying accusation she heard. God, she felt like a complete fool and there was no way she would tell him what happened between her and Master Greg, no way she'd let him know she made just as stupid a mistake by returning to Master Greg after she'd seen signs of his true nature as she had by running from him. Two erroneous judgements was at least one too many.

"I'm sorry. I don't know what happened. One minute I was fine, then I panicked because I couldn't move." That much was true. "I can't explain it." Okay, that wasn't, but it was the best she could do. "I'd like to go upstairs now, if that's all right."

"Come on then."

"No." Putting a hand on his chest, she looked up at him, saying, "You can stay. I'll be fine."

She was lying, both about her reason for her panic attack and that she'd be fine. She looked shell-shocked, fragile, and about ready to collapse. But now wasn't the time to push her for answers. Looking away from those drenched eyes, he saw Morgan approaching, Scott standing with Jack by the sofas. His friend knew what to do even if he didn't, he realized with relief.

"Here comes Morgan. It looks like she's ready to call it a night." Slipping his shirt back on her, he kissed her, adding, "We'll discuss this later."

CHAPTER TEN

Cassie kneaded the bread dough with strong squeezes, loving the feel of the soft, moist concoction in her hands. Humming under her breath, she basked in the work she loved and tried to forget the look of disappointment on Marc's face when she left the club room with Morgan last night. She woke this morning with a sore anus, a vivid reminder of his possession and the ultimate pleasure she derided from it, refusing to dwell on her ridiculous reaction to the sound of a cane being administered to a *willing* sub. If she had her way, that night would remain in her past never to be revisited again. Sex in public wasn't new to her, having indulged in exhibitionism with both Marc and Master Greg, but she'd never had anal sex with anyone. She'd always enjoyed anal play, but never took it any further. It felt right and fitting for Marc to be the one to breach her last virgin orifice.

Her buttocks clenched as she recalled the foreplay, both the pain and pleasure of it, that had been instrumental in helping her lower her inhibitions and relax enough to trust him with not only her body but her feelings. He kept her close to his side as she lay spooned against him all night, and remembering his concern and the tender way he held her after her 'episode' gave her hope his feelings were involved. Surely she had proven by now she was here to stay, that she wouldn't run from him and his domination. She didn't know what more she could do to prove she wanted to not only accept, but embrace his lifestyle.

Placing the dough in a deep-dish pan, she covered it with a towel then set it aside to rise before switching on the oven. She had several tins of muffins ready to go in along with four pies. There were a few things left from yesterday in her case out front, but that was it until she got her current dishes baked. After cleaning up, she checked the oven, frowning when she noticed it hadn't warmed up.

"Well, shit," she muttered after flipping the temp higher with still no heat. Her good mood took a sudden dive as she realized she would have to close the shop until she could get a new part, which could take until the first of next week. After placing a call to an appliance repairman, she waited on the few customers that stopped in before he arrived.

An hour later Cassie thanked the repairman after he assured her he would have a new heating element to her by Saturday morning. Now she debated whether to call Marc to return to town and pick her up or if she could grab a ride from Scott or one of his deputies. It was only mid-morning, and she knew he had a group to take out on the lake right after lunch. Picking up her phone, she hesitated, remembering Scott had been the first person she saw after Marc lifted her from the bench last night and the heated embarrassment flooding her face when she realized he witnessed her panic attack. Thankfully, he had been as supportive as Marc.

It would be silly to interrupt Marc again, so she pushed aside her embarrassment and pressed the sheriff's office number. After explaining the situation to the receptionist, Scott got on the phone and said he'd be right there.

After loading up her unbaked filled pans into a box to take to the lodge and bake there, she stepped out front in time for the sheriff to pull up. "That was quick," she said as he reached across the seat and opened the passenger door for her.

"I was on my way out to do patrols, so you had good timing. What's in the box?"

Setting it on the seat between them, she pulled her seat belt on. "My inventory for today that didn't get baked. This," she leaned down and lifted a brown sack from the box, "is for you. I hope you like snickerdoodles and raisin bread."

"I'm a guy, therefore easy. Enough said?" He turned a teasing grin on her as he pulled out and headed up to the lodge.

"Definitely enough said."

"Thanks for the goody bag. It wasn't necessary, but I'm not dumb enough to turn down homemade cookies and bread. Being a bachelor, I live on store bought and takeout. How long until your oven gets fixed?"

"Jimmy promised he'd have the part by closing tomorrow and installed first thing Saturday morning. I'll return tomorrow with these things and anything else I can get made in Marc's kitchen, but I'm apt to close early tomorrow also."

Cassie relaxed in her seat as Scott took a call on his radio, grateful for his laidback attitude and friendly chitchat making the ride back to the lodge comfortable. When he pulled up in front and opened his door to get out, she stopped him with a hand on his arm. "No, that's okay. I'm going right in. I appreciate the ride, sheriff."

He lifted his sunglasses to his head and gave her the direct look of a dom. "Did my presence last night demote me from friend to acquaintance?"

Damn her fair skin for reddening so easy, she swore as her face warmed under his close regard. "Uh, no, sorry, Scott."

"Good." Leaning over, he kissed her on the cheek then pushed her door open. "Thanks again for the goodies. If I gain weight, I'll know who to blame."

She thought of his lean, muscular build as she entered the lodge and imagined it would take more than a few baked goods to put any extra weight on him. Carrying her box, she trudged up the stairs, but slowed when she heard Marc's and Jack's voices.

"Hell, Marc, I hope you know what you're doing this time."

The hint of accusation in Jack's voice halted her on the top step and had her holding her breath as she listened closer.

"Relax," Marc answered, his tone easy. "I'm just doing an old friend a favor, that's all. Once it's done and the situation is resolved, I'm through. I'm not about to put myself through that again."

Was he talking about her, about the situation with her stalker? Had she pinned too much hope on his overprotective manner, the tender look she caught on occasion in his eyes when he didn't think she saw him? Pivoting on the top stair, she fled back down, tears of indecision clouding her vision so much she didn't see Morgan enter until she almost plowed into her.

"Cassie, what're you doing here?" Morgan asked before narrowing her eyes at her. "What's wrong?"

"What? Oh, nothing, Morgan, honest. I've just had a bad morning." She tried not to panic, struggled not to jump to conclusions like she had last time, but Marc's words refused to quit ringing in her ears, raising doubts. "Would you mind putting this in the kitchen? I'm going for a walk." Long walks always helped her clear her head.

"Sure," she said, taking the box. "Wait just a minute and I'll go with you."

"No! Sorry," she hastened to apologize when Morgan looked at her with suspicion. With Marc's words making her doubt his intentions, the last thing she needed was to see him right now. "I just need a little time to myself. Marc's been dogging my footsteps for days and it's driving me crazy." She plastered on her best reassuring smile, relieved when Morgan nodded.

"Follow that trail." She pointed out the open door and to the right. "Don't veer off it and you'll be able to keep the lodge in your sights and be within calling distance for about a mile. No further," she warned. "If you're not back in thirty minutes, I'm sending the guys after you and I can guarantee it won't be pleasant when they find you."

"I promise." Taking off before Morgan could change her mind and tell him where she was, she succeeded in holding tears of doubt and indecision at bay until she hit the trail. The dam burst as she moved into a sprint, as if she could run away from his hurtful words.

Remembering his unwelcoming reception when she first arrived, followed by his refusal to let her share his bed until she forced the issue, she lost the battle not to read anything personal into what she heard. She couldn't believe how stupid she was, how naïve she had been to think he would forget the past and welcome her back without reservations. Oh, she knew it wouldn't be easy, but after last night, she could've sworn he was with her because he wanted to be, not out of some misguided sense of obligation. With her head down and her vision blurred, she tried to flee the crushing pain sweeping through her, lost in her thoughts and her memories as she struggled to come to terms with her deflated hopes.

If only she hadn't panicked and shown that first note to the sheriff, she thought as her aimless wandering took her deeper into the dense forest. Would she have had another chance with him if Marc had accepted her back into his life, and his bed, on his own terms? She would never know because she blew that opportunity when she coerced her way back into his bed, never realizing how easy it would be for him to fuck her and then leave, much the same as she had done to him.

Only it hadn't been easy two years ago. Running from him had torn her up inside, left her to flounder alone, grappling with what she had done, had allowed him to do because of her fast escalating attachment to both the man and his domination. She spent weeks keeping to herself, never going out, avoiding her friends. Rick caught her at her lowest point when he asked her out. She accepted out of sheer desperation to replace memories of Marc with someone else, to prove she didn't want, didn't need the lifestyle he introduced her to. Another mistake in a long line of them.

She realized now the signs were all there only she had been too blind to see them. He never asked her personal questions, never took her anywhere, did nothing with her that didn't include sex or keeping an eye out for her stalker. She knew he didn't believe her lame excuse about her panic attack last night, but he hadn't even questioned her again this morning about it like she expected. He stuck close to make sure she stayed safe, not because he wanted her. Most dominant men were protective; he had been even when they first met. She knew now that didn't equate with stronger feelings or any desire to see their relationship evolve past sex.

Coming to a stop, she drew in a shaky breath, swiping at the tears running unchecked down her face before searching around the small glen until she spotted a grassy spot to sink down on. Leaning her head against a tree, she closed her eyes and wondered how she could have misread Marc's actions and those intent, probing looks so badly. Since the minute she arrived on his doorstep, unexpected and unannounced, he had done nothing to hint he wanted her gone. Oh, he hadn't been happy at first, but since she'd been with him every night for the past week, he'd seemed happy to have her here. If she had known he was just doing her a favor she never would have agreed to stay at the lodge with him.

With a deep sigh, Cassie worked to calm her rioting emotions before pushing to her feet. There was only one thing to do, she thought, resigned. She would pack her things and return to her apartment and maybe, given time, they could at least be friends again.

Heart heavy, she stood to head back the way she came when she realized the surrounding woods were so dense she couldn't see a shred of sunlight through them. An icy chill settled in her bones as she looked in every direction and saw with a sinking feeling she couldn't even make out the trail she had been following. On top of everything else that had gone wrong today, she let herself get so mired in grief, she got well and truly lost.

• • • • • • •

"Where'd this come from?" Marc asked Morgan when she entered the loft, her arms laden with canvas and paints.

Looking at the box she had set on the kitchen counter, Morgan checked her watch, blanching at the time. "Isn't Cassie back yet?"

Jack came out of the office, saw Morgan's pale, stricken face and rushed over to her. "What's wrong?"

"Cassie was here?" Marc asked at the same time, wondering what was going on. It wasn't anywhere near time for him to pick her up.

"I'm sorry, Marc. You know how I lose track of time when I'm painting. No excuse, I know, but I'm sure she's fine as I told her to stay on the north trail and within sight of the lodge."

His gut tightened in dread. She didn't know her way around these woods, had no clue about the perils lurking in the thick foliage despite doing his best to educate her the few times they had hiked. Glaring at Morgan, he snapped, "Back up, damn it. How long ago did she leave? What's she doing here at this time of day and how did she get here?" He had a bad feeling and worry over Cassie was at the root of it.

Morgan set her paints down, her brow furrowed in thought. "I don't know. I ran into her downstairs over two hours ago. She seemed really upset and asked if I'd set that box in the kitchen. I offered to go with her when she said she was going for a walk, but she wanted to be alone for a while."

"You said something that upset her?" Jack asked her, his eyes narrowed.

"Yes, but I don't know what."

Jack looked at Marc. "Two hours ago we were discussing you helping out Jason again. You don't think she misunderstood, do you?"

Marc tried to remember what he said. Jason Davies, a friend from their Army days who had saved his ass one night when a group of them went off base to a bar while stationed overseas and Marc got jumped, hadn't fared well since leaving the military. On and off drugs for years, Jason had called him a few times to bail him out of jail or help him get into rehab. He had gotten a call from him that morning and planned on making one more trip to Denver on his friend's behalf. Hell, he had even thought about asking Cassie to accompany him, the first time he'd considered testing their relationship beyond sex. It would have also given him an opportunity to grill her again about the root of her panic attack last night, the one that took ten years off his life. Recalling the short conversation, he couldn't imagine why anything they said would have upset her. He mentioned Jason's name, but since she didn't know him that wouldn't have meant anything.

Anger joined the worry churning in his abdomen. Just as he had grilled into her the first time they met about the importance of open communication, he had emphasized several times the dangers of going into the woods alone. "I can't fathom why our conversation would have upset her, but she knew better than to take off alone. Between her panic attack last night, which I haven't had time to get to the bottom of, and now this little stunt, that woman has taken ten years off my life." He ignored Jack's smirk as he paced. "I swear, she won't sit down for a week when I get through with her. Hell, she's been gone two fucking hours.

She could be anywhere." Picturing her lost, alone, and afraid had him breaking out in a cold sweat. There were numerous hazards that could befall an inexperienced hiker unfamiliar with this area.

"God, Marc, I'm so sorry." Morgan had tears in her eyes as she saw the worry reflected on both their faces.

"You call Scott, I'll round up our guests and get a search party going." Jack took Morgan's hand and turned to go.

"I'll start out on the way she went. Keep in touch." He followed them down the stairs, pressing Scott's number as he went. A few minutes later he had the whole story of why she returned to the lodge this morning and a promise from Scott he'd be here to help as soon as possible. Hastening down the trail Cassie had taken, he alternated between cursing her for her rash flight and praying for her safety.

Traipsing through the woods he knew like the back of his hand, he had time to think with a more rational head and admit to his own mistakes, even though his anger simmered over her blatant disregard of his number one rule. From the moment she walked into the lodge and looked at him with such naked longing out of those big blue eyes, he'd refused to think of her as anything but an old acquaintance, a former sub, fuck buddy, whatever label he could think of instead of the one woman who always meant more than any other.

He hadn't wanted to go down that road with her again, couldn't trust that she wouldn't bail if his lifestyle became too much for her to handle. If she had just stayed and talked to him that night when she looked at him with stunned betrayal in her eyes, he would've sat down with her and discussed her misgivings, her fears and concerns. And if she still hadn't wanted to be shared, he would have respected her wishes. But she had run and refused every attempt he made to get hold of her over the next few days.

Living in such close quarters with Jack and Morgan the past six months, seeing how rewarding a committed relationship could be with the right person, had driven home how much he wanted the same thing. He made a mistake keeping their relationship strictly sexual once Cassie finagled her way out to the lodge and into his bed. He never would have given in to her had his feelings not already been leaning toward giving her another chance.

"Marc!"

"Over here." He stopped on the trail and waited for Scott to catch up.

"No sign of her?" Scott asked, meeting up with him at a fork between three trails.

"No. I found where she veered off the trail though and I think I'm on the right track." Anger and worry colored his voice as he paused and looked ahead through the dense woods. "Son of a bitch, I'm going to blister her ass when I find her," he swore as the two of them set out again together.

"I'll help you. What made her take off? I thought she had a lot of baking to do at your place."

"I'm not sure, but whatever it was doesn't excuse her rash behavior." Pausing, he took a deep breath, trying to quell the panic threatening his composure. "Hell, I've made a few mistakes, avoided talking about our relationship or any kind of future."

"Are you glad she's here?" Scott asked him in his direct way, his gray eyes shifting from their path to gaze at him.

"Yeah, yeah, I am. I wanted the girl the minute I saw her two years ago and nothing has changed since. If anything, I want her more now than I did back then. It took a hell of a lot of guts to travel here, start a new business, and look me up without knowing whether she'd be welcome. Gotta admire her determination, even if it put me on the spot at first."

Holding back a large tree limb, Scott smiled. "Then let's go find her."

· · · · · · ·

Thirty minutes later, relief at hearing Cassie's voice

returning their calls threatened to weaken his knees. Moving faster, they burst into a small clearing to find her leaning against a tree, tired and worried but unharmed.

"At least you had the good sense to stay put when you found yourself lost," Marc growled, his relief at finding her safe mixed with his anger for the grief she caused him.

Cassie stood, wishing she could fling herself into his arms, the relief sweeping through her at being found making her knees weak. But she didn't have that right and the anger in his tone and swirling in his green eyes didn't bode well for gaining any sympathy. Wary of facing two angry, dominant men, she had a sinking feeling she was in for another spanking, one that might not be as erotic as the others. Then she remembered his words to Jack and her own ire stirred.

"I'm not completely stupid," she bit out, "except where you're concerned."

Marc saw Scott's smile before he stepped away and pulled out his pager to let Jack and the others know they could call off the search and head back home. With slow precision, he advanced toward her, striving to keep his anger in check. She looked tired and strained, a reminder of how she must have been scared out of her wits out here alone for the past two hours.

"Before you explain that statement, tell me if you're all right." he asked in a softer tone when he reached her. "Here." Handing her a bottle of water, he looked her over while she downed it, assuring himself she was unharmed.

"Thank you, and yes, I'm fine. I'm sorry I bothered everyone. I didn't mean to get lost."

"Nobody means to get lost, darlin', but if you ignore the basic rules of hiking in these mountains, it's bound to happen. Rules I believe I told you about before our hike the other day."

Cassie wondered how far she'd get playing the 'poor me' act, then looked at his face and knew she may as well not bother. He looked well and truly pissed. Maybe if she explained he'd understand, but the thought of telling him she thought she meant more to him than she apparently did had her cringing in humiliation. "Can we go back now? I have a lot of work to do, that is if I can use your kitchen," she said, hoping he'd let the rule thing slide.

"No, we can't go back now. First, I'm going to show you how I deal with rule-breaking from my sub. Then, on the long trek back, you can explain yourself." Grabbing her hand as she took a hasty step back, he pulled her to him, turning to see where Scott went. Always thinking ahead, his friend had already removed his belt.

"I decided you were too upset to mete it out, so I'll do it for you," he stated when Marc raised an eyebrow at him.

"You're right."

"Right about what?" Cassie looked from Scott and the wide leather belt looped over in his hand to Marc, a shiver of apprehension rippling up her spine as she imagined the sting from that leather strap.

"That I'm too put out with you at the moment to discipline you myself, so Scott will do it."

"No. You can spank me later, when you're not upset." She tried to pull away from him, but his grip remained tight. While a part of her mind panicked over the thought of Scott using his belt on her, another part, the part she labeled her secret, slutty Marc part, was excited about the prospect. The erotic pain from her previous spankings always led to powerful orgasms, as did being observed. But this time would be for punishment and not with Scott watching, but meting it out. Before she could assimilate how she felt about that, Marc had her jeans shoved down and a hard arm wrapped around her waist as he bent her over. "Wait, Marc! Please!" She tried to struggle, but a hard slap on her bare ass put a quick stop to it.

"No, I will not wait. You took off alone." The belt snapped across her buttocks and she yelped at the fiery pain. "And you didn't stay within sight of the lodge," he continued, reaching under her with his free hand and cupping her unfettered breast beneath her shirt as Scott smacked her again. "And you have explaining to do as to why."

The belt stroked across her vulnerable buttocks again and she bit her lip as he continued to torment her, the slapping flesh snap of leather against her bottom echoing in the mountain air. Marc's confusion over her reason for taking off had her wondering if she heard him wrong.

The new hope blossoming in her chest helped her accept her punishment and the accompanying pain. Her buttocks throbbed with the scorching burn and she knew right away she wouldn't find any pleasure with this spanking. His hand on her breast soothed rather than stimulated and went a long way toward helping her bear the consequences of her actions. As if the humiliation of being bent over bare assed and punished by Scott wasn't enough, guilt over the trouble she caused everyone ate at her conscience. Sitting wouldn't be an option by the time the sheriff finished belaboring her butt.

A pathetic, mewling cry escaped her compressed lips when he shifted his aim to the under curve of her cheeks and then the tops of her thighs. She tried to remain stoic and accept her punishment, but the sharp strokes on that ultra-sensitive skin had her kicking out, trying to shift her hips away from the descending belt.

"She reddens to a beautiful shade," Scott said as he landed another blow right on top of a previous one and then ran his hand over her abused flesh. "You didn't set a number, so, unless you want bruises, I'm done."

Marc frowned, glancing at her ass. While it was red and puffy, he knew Scott wouldn't leave bruises any more than he would. He left the softness of her breast to join in caressing her hot buttocks. "I think she's had enough." Her low moan and slight lift of her hips toward their hands changed their frowns of displeasure to smirks.

"She likes to be petted," Scott drawled then stopped her shifting buttocks by kneading the plump warm flesh.

"*Ow!*" Cassie cried out with the tight squeeze of her right cheek. "I thought you'd finished!" She should have scrambled to lift herself from Marc's hold, but in truth, she enjoyed both men's attention, their soft caresses exciting her until one of them had been callous enough to add to her discomfort and stopped her budding arousal.

Chuckling, Scott slapped her cheek then put his belt back on. "I'll let you finish this how you see fit and see you later."

Marc lifted her up, wiped the tears from her cheeks then ordered in a soft, implacable voice that had her leaning into him, "Cassie, kiss Scott and thank him for punishing you for me."

Her face flaming as hot as her butt, she turned to the other man, relaxing when she looked into his sparkling eyes. He made it easier by holding out his arms and hugging her before she lifted her head away from the steady beat of his heart under her ear. "Thank you, sir." Reaching up, she laid her lips on his. When he deepened the kiss, opening her mouth and stroking her tongue with his, she leaned into his hard chest and clasped his shoulders in a tight grip. *Damn, the man can kiss*, she thought as he explored her mouth and lips with leisurely thoroughness, his hands caressing her buttocks now with soft strokes, stirring her arousal again. Disappointment surprised her when he ended the kiss, removed his hands, and turned her back to Marc.

"Later, sweetie." He grinned down at her, tapping her nose before striding off.

When she turned questioning blue eyes up to Marc, he pulled up her jeans, asking, "You ready to run?"

Enlightenment dawned as she realized there had been a second reason he allowed Scott to administer her punishment. He needed to know if she'd accept the other man's touch. "No, I'm not going to run."

"Tell me why you took off the way you did." Taking her hand, he started the trek back to the lodge, intending to take that time to get a few things straight with her.

Glad for the narrow trail that forced them to walk single file for now, she found it easier to answer him without those probing green eyes on her. "I heard you tell Jack you were just doing a favor for a friend and that you would be through with me once you resolved the problem." She shrugged even though he didn't look back. When he didn't respond, she gave his back an exasperated look and tugged on their hands.

Glancing around, he didn't smile at her scowl, but he wanted to. Raising a brow, he asked, "And?"

"And I thought, I had hoped we were moving toward a relationship that meant more than sex. There, are you happy now?" she snapped.

Marc stopped walking, turned and pulled her to him. "We are much more than fuck buddies, something you would know if you had listened to our whole conversation or come to me instead of running away, again."

"I…"

"Quiet. I was speaking of a favor I intend to do for a friend next week, a friend I've helped in the past and have realized he's using me as a crutch. Therefore, it will be the last time I help him out of this particular kind of bind."

"Oh. I'm sorry." Cassie narrowed her eyes at him, needing, wanting more than that now. "And how was I supposed to know that?"

Resuming walking, he tossed over his shoulder, "You assumed I had no interest in you other than seeing you safe from your stalker and sex. I admit it pissed me off the way you blindsided me with your sudden appearance and I didn't handle our reunion too well, and I apologize for that." Exiting the woods into the lodge's back yard, he turned to her with a scowl. "But make no mistake, darlin', *no one* can coerce me into something I don't want to do. If I didn't care about you, how do I know you applied to substitute teach or you befriended Ed the first day you opened the bakery?"

The surprise on her face reinforced his guilt. All the signs were there, staring him in the face he still wanted more from her, just like he had when they first met, only he'd been too annoyed to see them. She went to extremes to return to him, hoping for the best; he should've been more open to meeting her halfway.

Stifling the urge to grin at her shocked, bemused look, he said, "We'll finish discussing our relationship later. Today, I have to see to our guests since we had to cancel their plans in order to look for you."

"I said I was sorry," she grumbled, still grappling with his confession. "Thank you for finding me."

"Can't lose my favorite girl, now can I? I gotta go. I'll expect a pie or something after dinner."

"I can do that." Smiling, Cassie trotted upstairs to catch up on her baking.

CHAPTER ELEVEN

Saturday morning, Marc dropped Cassie off at the bakery an hour earlier than usual so she could meet Jimmy and get her oven going again. After setting out the items she baked at the lodge yesterday afternoon and evening, she got to work preparing concoctions for the weekend regulars and the personal orders she'd received. Opening the now toasty warm oven, she removed a large pan of brownies and slid another inside when the front door chimes pealed, signaling a customer.

"Be right with you," she called out.

"It's just me, dear," Ed answered. "I'll set your mail on the counter."

Hurrying out front, she caught him before he left. "Wait, Ed, I've got a cherry tart for you." As she handed him a small bag containing his treat, Ed beamed at her.

"You spoil me, but I'm not complaining. Have a nice weekend. I'll see you Monday."

"You too." Picking up the mail, she flipped through it, her pleasant mood taking a nose dive when she saw the plain white envelope with no return address. With shaking hands, she slit it open and shook it, not wanting to touch anything. A picture slid out face up. Nausea churned inside her, threatening to come up as she stared down at a photo of herself bent over Marc's arm, her bare ass on display for Scott standing to her side, the belt hanging from his hand, a picture perfect explanation for the redness covering her buttocks and thighs. Just the thought of this person out there with her, close enough to take this picture, close enough to harm either one of the men, was enough to make her want to run and hide. But she refused to do that. With the slow tightening of her muscles, anger overrode her fear and had her reaching for the phone.

Scott arrived under ten minutes later, his gray eyes snapping with ire as he looked down at the photo. "No note?" he asked, looking up at her pale but composed face, admiring the way she held herself together.

"No, just the picture." The picture would have embarrassed her if having her privacy invaded hadn't angered her so much. She clenched her hands as the sense of violation constricted her throat. She had loved playing with Marc in the woods and now that pleasure had been tarnished for her.

Using his pen, the sheriff flipped the picture over, revealing the message:

You Should Have Listened Now You'll Pay

"Shit. You don't make a move without someone with you, got it?"

Cassie could see why he made a good dom. She wasn't about to argue with him. "I won't, I promise."

Slipping the photo into a plastic bag, he told her, "I'm calling Marc and have him get out here to stay until you close. Don't worry, sweetie, we'll catch this guy."

She knew he meant to reassure her with his smile, but her tense shoulders didn't relax. Nodding, she returned to the kitchen. Things were going so well between her and Marc and now this. She wished whoever he was would make a play for her. At least then this waiting on pins and needles would be over.

Scott stayed until Marc arrived. One look at the picture had him swearing and threatening this guy with a slow and painful death. Thinking of Cassie alone in the woods with this pervert somewhere nearby jeopardized his control, had his vision going red with promised retribution and he vowed to stick to her like glue until they caught the bastard.

"You coming out to the lodge tonight?" he asked Scott when Cassie went into the kitchen and out of earshot.

"I planned on it. What'd you have in mind?"

"Something to take her mind off this son of a bitch." It had been late last night by the time he and Jack got caught up with their guests and he spent the remainder of the night lying in bed, holding her close and wishing he could have gotten free sooner so they could talk more. Now his anger and his cock demanded he stake his claim, once again offer her the ultimate in satisfaction by allowing another to join them, and hope he wasn't pushing too fast again.

"I think I can be available to help with that. It's lingerie night, right?"

"Yes, our favorite theme." He smiled, thinking of the outfit he bought for her to wear tonight.

"I look forward to seeing her in whatever has you smiling. Meanwhile, I'll ask around about strangers in the area, but I doubt if that'll turn up any clues."

"Thanks, Scott. We'll check with our guests too. Most of them we know, so we'll ask them about any of these new players. We'll get him." Marc was sure of that, he just hoped it was soon and before he could hurt Cassie. Now he had found her again, he wasn't about to lose her.

• • • • • • •

Cassie perused the small package on the bed with a wary eye. Marc informed her all the women are expected to wear lingerie tonight, and he had bought her something special. Special meant provocative, she thought as she lifted the lid off the small white box. Then again, anything in the box would be more coverage than naked, which she assumed she would be at some point. A blue satin demi bra with white lace trim and matching thong lay nestled in the tissue paper. Lifting the bra, she thought it the prettiest set she had ever seen.

She looked up when he came in, the look in his eyes as he strode over to her and removed the damp towel covering her flushed body setting all her girly parts to tingling.

"The blue matches your eyes."

"It's lovely, Marc. Thank you." Slipping on the bra, she turned so he could hook it. Looking down, it ruffled her to see the cups were only big enough to provide a shelf for her breasts, plumping them up, leaving her bare nipples protruding out.

"Perfect."

Before she could complain, he leaned down and drew one soft peak into his mouth. Cassie leaned into him, her embarrassment taking second place to the pleasure of his mouth suckling her. "Marc, master, do we have to go downstairs right now?" she moaned, wanting nothing more than for him to toss her on the bed and fuck her hard.

He took his time, releasing her nipple with a strong pull before smiling at her. His intention to erase the worried look on her face succeeded; the tight, pinched lines around her eyes and mouth relaxed, her eyes reflecting low arousal. "Yes, we do. Now hold still, darlin'." Withdrawing a small object from his pocket, he clamped the nipple ring around her distended bud then loosened it a touch before drawing her other nipple into his mouth to ready it for the matching clamp.

Even though she knew what to expect, she still had to suck in a much-needed breath against the sharp bite of pain then released it on a whoosh as it subsided to a soft pulse.

"Slip these on and we'll head down."

Cassie stepped into the thong, bracing her hands on his shoulders while trying to ignore the way the chain attached to the two nipple rings swayed and pulled on her sensitive tips.

Catching her grimace, Marc kissed her. "Don't worry, you won't have to wear them long."

"From what I remember, it hurts worse when they come off than when they go on."

He just smiled, took her hand, and led her out of the room. Morgan and Jack were coming out of their room and Jack took his time looking her over before winking at her, causing her face to heat even more.

"Very pretty, Cassie."

Turning away from his intent, yet teasing gaze, she glanced at Morgan. Dressed in a calf-length, see-through ivory gown, it was obvious she wore nothing underneath it.

"Morgan, you look innocent and seductive. Good choice, Jack," Marc commented.

"Why do I feel more naked wearing this than I would naked?" Morgan asked of no one in particular as they headed downstairs.

"I don't know, princess. Would you rather I slipped it off now before we go in?" Jack asked her.

"No, sir." Morgan glanced at Cassie and rolled her eyes.

Giggling, she followed Marc into the club room, glad to see only one other couple had arrived. Jack fixed them a drink, then they left her and Morgan seated at the bar while they greeted their guests and mingled. As others arrived, she and Morgan found themselves grateful for their meager outfits. Most of the women wore gowns with holes cut out for breasts and pussies or bras and panties with similar cut-outs. At least she was starting the night partly clothed, she thought, looking down at her cupped breasts and pinched nipples.

Loud, pulsating music along with low-pitched laughter resonated around the room as others joined them and Cassie enjoyed people watching as she finished her drink. This group seemed comfortable with each other and eager to play. Squirming on the stool, she couldn't look away when two women seemed more than happy to kneel before a seated man and lower their mouths to share his cock. The woman seated next to him had her legs draped over a man's shoulders as he knelt in front of her and buried his head between them while she played with her breasts.

"Eager, aren't they?" Morgan asked as they both watched.

"I'll say." Taking a deep breath, she turned to her new friend and sought her advice. "I think Marc has plans to invite someone to join us tonight. It didn't bother you when Jack shared you?" Old insecurities were sneaking up on her, but they weren't as forceful as the first time and she wouldn't let them ruin everything she risked so much for. But a little reassurance would be welcome.

"The first time was with Marc and I had reservations, but after I experienced four hands and two mouths intent on nothing but my pleasure, I gotta tell you, there's nothing like it. If it helps, Jack's only allowed Marc and Scott to join us and limited their participation to oral, and that was only if I agreed, which, as you know, I did."

Ignoring the twinge of jealousy at the reminder of Marc's involvement with the other couple, Cassie saw nothing but honesty on Morgan's face and the remembrance of exalted pleasure reflected in her eyes. "Most men would be jealous if someone else touched the woman they cared about," she couldn't help but point out.

"They aren't most men." Morgan shrugged, glanced across the room where Jack conversed with a couple, and her heart gave that sudden lurch it always did when she looked at him. Smiling, she stated, "His main focus since I showed up on his doorstep last winter has been on looking out for me, just like always." Turning back to Cassie, she added in all honesty, "I wouldn't trade that for anything."

Cassie nodded, hearing loud and clear what she said. A few minutes later, both women had their eyes on Scott when he entered and strode over to them with a loose-limbed stride and a wicked gleam in his eyes.

"God, he's hot," Cassie whispered.

"Don't I know it, girlfriend."

"Good evening, ladies."

Tugging on Cassie's chain, he bent and gave Morgan a light kiss. She struggled not to yelp at the sudden jolt the chain gave her nipples that zeroed straight down to her clit. If she wasn't so crazy in love with Marc, she suspected she could fall for the sheriff. He had that whole dom thing down pat. Combined with his attractive, rugged features and easygoing demeanor, he'd make any woman's heart and core throb. Although he wielded a nasty belt, as her still sore butt could attest to.

"Where is Master Marc, Cassie?"

"Right here." Marc slipped his hands around her waist and lifted her off the stool. "It's about time you got here. The bench is clear." Looking down at her, he held her against him with an arm around her waist and tipped her chin up with his free hand. "Scott and I are going to scene with you, darlin'. Are you okay with that?"

She experienced none of the sense of betrayal she had the last time he arranged a ménage. Even though he hadn't said the words, his actions, notably in the past few days, all spoke of caring and a commitment to keeping her happy, and if that commitment included the ultimate sexual experience of two men, she would no longer deny him or herself that pleasure.

"I'm okay with it."

Cupping her face in his hands, he kissed her. "I love you, darlin'." He hastened to lay a finger across her lips before she could reply. "Tell me later, after."

Bemused as well as shaken by his words, she followed him to the front of the room where a padded, waist-high bench similar to the spanking bench stood unoccupied. They both were silent as Marc removed her bra while Scott slipped her thong off, leaving her naked except for the nipple rings.

"Up you go, sweetie." Scott lifted her onto the bench

and eased her back before strapping her wrists down at her sides. "Relax. We'll be right here with you," he said when she struggled against the restraints.

Cassie tried to relax as they each grabbed an ankle, bent her legs and strapped her down with her knees spread. When Marc pulled a strap across her hips, leaving her unable to move at all, her sheath moistened in anticipation, her breathing growing labored.

"I'm going to blindfold you." He showed her the black blindfold he had put on her before. "It will heighten your senses. You won't have to think about who is doing what, just lie there and enjoy." He hesitated a moment then bent and asked with quiet emphasis, "Are you *really* going to be okay with this? Not thinking of panicking again on me, are you? Because I don't think my heart could take a repeat, darlin'. You scared the crap out of me the other night and we haven't had a chance to discuss that." He needed to get to the bottom of that as soon as her stalker has been found and locked up. In an area with a constant, steady flow of tourists coming and going, it was damn difficult to look for a stranger intent on harm.

"I'm good, master, I promise." The only shivers rippling under her skin tonight were from anticipation and excitement, making it easy for her to lift her head so he could tie the blindfold behind her. Now nothing but music and the sounds of slapping flesh and cries of pleasure surrounded her, the warm lights shining above her and hands running over her body the only things she felt.

Lips and tongues caressed her clamped nipples, the dual stimulation sending her blood pressure skyrocketing. *Oh, God.* Pain blossomed with the removal of the clamps, the sudden rush of blood flow leaving her gasping for breath. Two pairs of lips wrapped around each throbbing tip, easing the pain along with the soothing strokes of their tongues until they had her aching for more.

She forgot about the party going on around them, heard nothing but Marc's and Scott's deep voices whispering praise in her ears as they pleasured her. Within minutes, she discovered being the sole object of their attention was a heady experience she'd been foolish to run from. Lips touched hers—Marc's, because she'd know his lips anywhere—while hard hands plumped and kneaded her breasts.

"You are exquisite in your passion," he whispered against her mouth before tracing her lips with his tongue then moving down her neck.

"I agree." Scott's mouth took the place of Marc's and Cassie fell into his kiss, enjoying his taste and his hands as they glided over her.

She whimpered when he moved away then gasped as their hands and mouths traced her body with slow exploration, suckling her tortured nipples again before licking and nipping their way down her stomach to her mound. She lost track of whose mouth and hands were whose and succumbed to the pleasure they induced. Lips caressed her damp folds as fingers spread them, exposing her very core, leaving them no illusions as to her eager acceptance of their touch.

When more than one finger penetrated the moist depths of her pussy, Cassie's cry rent the air, her attempt to arch into the thrusts failing, frustrating and arousing her at the same time. Her helplessness added to the exalted pleasure as the darkness behind her blindfold burst into a kaleidoscope of colors when they brought her to one orgasm after another. With fingers, lips, and tongues they left no inch of her untouched, deep thrusts into her sheath and anus had her screaming in response, soft strokes from their tongues over her swollen needy clit had her moaning and jerking with wave after wave of ecstasy. One peak would end only to herald the onset of another. One of them moved back up to her breasts and with perfect coordination she found her nipple sucked along with her clit, the overwhelming sensations tossing her into another rioting storm of pleasure.

With what seemed like hours later, Cassie lay panting and shaken, her body coated with a sheen of perspiration, her nipples and clit aching and sore from so much attention and so many climaxes. With the lift of her blindfold, she stared up into the smiling green eyes she loved so much.

"Master."

Her soft, sated voice was music to Marc's ears, her flushed face beautiful to his eyes, her trembling body soft under his hands. Releasing the straps, he teased, "Darlin'. I don't think I have to ask if you enjoyed yourself."

"No, you don't have to ask." Sitting up with their help, she blinked a few times as her eyes adjusted to her surroundings. She saw people smiling and moving away from their scene area, but didn't have the energy to get embarrassed over what they saw and heard. She spotted Morgan on her right, tethered on the St. Andrew's cross, her body shuddering under the onslaught of Jack's possession. Her gaze shifted to Marc and Scott and their undeniable erections. "Um, what about you, sir? Don't you want to…"

"Most definitely we want to," Marc answered, his grin wicked when she floundered. He'd have to remember how multiple orgasms left her so flustered. "Come with us, Cassie. We'll go someplace a little more private."

They each took her hands and led her outside to the whirlpool. The evening had cooled, as it does in the mountains even in summer months, and goosebumps rose on her bare, damp skin.

"You look cold, sweetie. In you go." With a hand on her butt, Scott guided her down into the heated, swirling water.

She leaned back and watched in appreciation as both men stripped and joined her, their jutting erections already seeping. When they stood in front of her, she needed no encouragement to lean forward and take Marc's cock into her mouth while gripping Scott's with her hand. Their deep moans added to her pleasure, sounded loud with only the occasional hoot from an owl to disturb the quiet night as she alternated sucking and stroking each of them, taking her time to find their pleasure spots and concentrate on those areas to drive them as crazy as they had her.

She already knew Marc liked having the underside of his cock head licked and discovered Scott enjoyed a tight grip around his shaft. Both men loved the swirl of her tongue over their slit and her hands cupping their balls. Cassie was enjoying herself so much, she protested when they pulled away from her and Marc lifted her onto the padded edge of the tub.

"As much as we were enjoying that, darlin', we have other plans for you." With a hand between her breasts, he pushed her back to brace herself on her arms.

Without giving her time to wonder what they had in mind, Scott moved behind her, tilted her head back and straddled her face. Opening for his cock, she took him deep, relieved he kept hold of the base of his dick to keep from choking her. Marc lifted her legs, draping them over his broad shoulders before he gripped her buttocks and plunged balls deep inside her. She felt every ridge of his bare cock as he stroked her slick walls, and she relished gaining his trust even as she bemoaned the time it took. Moaning around the hard shaft filling her mouth, she accepted their thrusts, her body coming alive again with each deep stroke and the knowledge of Marc's trust.

This time the men concentrated on their own pleasure, but she had no trouble becoming aroused and joining them. With grunts and groans, the two of them used her body for their satisfaction and she gladly accepted their possession of her. Scott came first, his come shooting down her throat as his rigid length jerked in her mouth with his shout of release. Cassie lifted her head as he pulled out of her mouth and braced herself against Marc's increasing thrusts. With her legs draped over his shoulders and her butt elevated by his hands, she could do nothing but take his assault and enjoy the climax she felt coming on. Face as hard as his cock, he kept his gaze glued to their joined bodies as he brought them both to a shattering climax.

Cassie sank back into the whirlpool, sighing as the warm water flowed around her aching body and lulled her into complacency. With the men seated on each side of her, she rested her head back on Marc's arm and started to drift off when a voice she recognized startled all three of them.

"I warned you to come back to me, Cassie."

Incredulous, she jerked upright, swiveling around to stare in shock at the man holding a gun on the three of them. "Greg?"

• • • • • • •

Jack looked around the club room again then sought Jake Combs, the one who booked this group and knew everyone, his sixth sense kicking in big time. Spotting him on a sofa with his sub, he grabbed Morgan's hand and made his way to him.

"What's wrong?" Morgan asked, knowing when Jack was worried.

"I need to check on someone. Jake," he said, stopping in front of the other couple. "I need a word with you about Mason Gregory."

"Who?" Jake asked as he rose to speak with him.

"A guy named Mason Gregory checked in Wednesday, after all of you, but I haven't seen him since. What do you know about him?"

"Nothing. I've never heard of anyone by that name. He must have learned about our trip from someone else and wheedled in on our reservations. I'm sorry, Jack."

"Shit. Keep an eye on things in here, will you? I've got to find Marc." Jack turned to Morgan, his face tight with worry. "Stay here and don't budge until I return." Hurrying upstairs, he looked for Marc, finding him when he glanced out the window to check the hot tub. Swearing a blue streak, he grabbed the rifle he used to scare off bears and for protection. Cursing for not listening to the warning bells ringing in his head all evening as he checked off everyone showing up for the party and never saw Mason Gregory, he ran back downstairs and out the front so he could come up on them unawares.

• • • • • • •

"Greg, what are you doing?"

Marc and Scott had risen and eyed the threat to them, their low curses rife with anger for letting their guard down. "Do you know this idiot, Cassie?" Marc didn't bother masking his derision, his gaze cool on the blond-haired man.

"I was her master until she betrayed me." He drilled Cassie with a glacial look. "Wade blackballed me from all clubs after your little temper tantrum over the cane. You'll pay for that and for not heeding my warnings to come back to me."

"You? You're my stalker?" Cassie rose, uncaring about her nudity as she stared at him in disbelief, finding it hard to believe she made such an impression on him or he'd blame her for ignoring her safeword. "I said cherry over and over, but you ignored me!" she exclaimed in outrage. "You deserved to be tossed out of there." She didn't know where her bravado came from because inside she quaked so hard she felt sick with fear. Maybe being flanked by two men who outweighed Greg helped lend her the courage she needed to face her tormentor. She had cowered away from this man once; she refused to let him see her that way again.

"Cassie."

She ignored Marc's warning, intent on holding her own. "Greg, I told you up front I wanted Marc, it was him I was there to learn for," she stated, ignoring the tight squeeze Marc gave her arm as he shoved her behind him then released her to shield her with his body planted in front of her.

"I don't care what you told me. Come here, Cassie." Greg aimed the gun at Marc. "Or your boyfriend gets the first bullet."

"No! I'll come with you." Panic and insurmountable fear for both Marc and Scott enabled her to dart around them before either could stop her. Stepping out of the tub, shaking from the cool air and terror, she took one shaky step toward him before her nerve deserted her and left her rooted in place.

"Cassie, get away from him," Marc snapped, swearing when she agilely evaded his reach, trying to figure out if he could rush this guy and give Scott a chance to get to his gun by his clothes, where he was already inching toward.

Greg reached forward, grabbed Cassie, and pulled her in front of him. Putting the gun to her head, he gripped her breast with his free hand and squeezed.

Cassie bit her lip and Marc growled. He would take this bastard apart with his bare hands for causing her distress. With relief, he noticed Jack sneaking up behind Greg, his rifle cocked and ready.

"You're awfully brave with a woman as a shield," Marc taunted, stepping out of the tub, preparing to go for this guy as soon as he got the chance.

"Shut up, asshole. I ought to take you out for fucking her, but I need to get going. Come after us and I'll put a bullet in both of you."

"You're not going anywhere. Drop it and let her go." Jack poked the rifle into the guy's back while using his free hand to remove the gun from his grip. As soon as he had it, Marc charged him, shoving Cassie toward Jack as he landed a hard blow to Greg's stomach followed by a sharp uppercut to his jaw. It didn't surprise him to see him drop and curl into a ball. The guy bullied only those weaker than him, like innocent subs who should have been able to trust him. Picturing Cassie tied, crying out her safeword in fear and pain and being ignored had him leaning down and lifting Greg's head by his hair to deliver another solid blow to his not so pretty face. "That was for my sub."

Scott moved fast to cuff him before scowling at Marc. "You had to go and deck him again, didn't you?"

"If I hadn't, you would have."

"Exactly. You got all the fun." Scott got dressed and hauled Greg off, leaving Cassie in Marc's arms.

"I'll leave you two alone," Jack said with a wink at Cassie's wide-eyed look.

"I owe you, Jack. Thanks." Marc hugged her shaking body tighter when she turned her face into his shoulder and wept.

"No, you don't," he replied. "You forget, I know what she means to you."

Gripping her upper arms, he moved her back just far enough to growl, "Want to tell me what the fuck you were trying to prove just now? I *told* you to stay back."

Cocking her head, her simple answer all but floored him. "I knew you wouldn't let anything happen to me."

Closing his eyes against the proof of her trust shining on her open face, he hauled her against him, not even trying to disguise his shaken voice as he whispered, "Do you have any idea what you mean to me?"

"Maybe as much as you mean to me, Marc. I love you."

"I've waited a long time to hear those words, darlin'. You might have to say them a lot to make up for lost time."

Cassie beamed up at him. "I can do that."

THE END

STORMY NIGHT PUBLICATIONS WOULD LIKE TO THANK YOU FOR YOUR INTEREST IN OUR BOOKS.

If you liked this book (or even if you didn't), we would really appreciate you leaving a review on the site where you purchased it. Reviews provide useful feedback for us and for our authors, and this feedback (both positive comments and constructive criticism) allows us to work even harder to make sure we provide the content our customers want to read.

If you would like to check out more books from Stormy Night Publications, if you want to learn more about our company, or if you would like to join our mailing list, please visit our website at:

www.stormynightpublications.com

Manufactured by Amazon.ca
Bolton, ON